JAR OF HEARTS

LISA HUGHEY

JAR OF HEARTS

A Family Stone Novella
by Lisa Hughey

May 2014

Lisa Hughey

Jar of Hearts ISBN: 978-0-9903793-0-0

Print ISBN: 978-0-9991951-5-4

 Created with Vellum

"Keisha!" Jack Stone shouted from his office.

Sheesh. "Hold your damn horses, Jack," Keisha shouted right back but she also didn't dally at her desk once she heard his bellow.

She wanted to kick herself. She'd been so threatened by the fact that her boss Jack had hired not one, but two, new employees, Jess and Colin, that she'd tried to hold too tight to control during the Port-du-Bois mission. Luckily in the end it had all turned out okay, but if they had been unsuccessful, the bulk of the failure would have rested with her. So now every time Jack shouted at her from his office, a little niggle of worry followed. Perhaps today was the day he was going to fire her.

Dammit, Keish, why can't you trust more easily?

Keisha rolled her eyes at Ava Sanchez, Jack's assistant, as she passed her desk. Ava just smiled serenely as Keisha pushed open the door to his office.

"Yes, *sir?*" she replied sharply and fought the urge to salute Jack. Always the smart ass. So hard to turn it off even when she knew the term of authority annoyed Jack.

"Cut that out." Jack twirled his finger indicating she should shut the door. "And come on in."

Her heart thundered in her chest. She'd been waiting for the hammer to come down on her since that op. It had been a little crazy around the office with all the Stone family siblings hooking up during the holidays. But in the back of her mind, she'd been expecting to get reamed for the mistakes she made on the island.

She loved this job. She did not want to lose it. But instead of adopting a quiet subservient demeanor, she flipped on her 'I don't give a damn' attitude and shut the door with a snick. If she was getting fired, no way was she going to let him know how much that upset her. She'd learned at a young age not to show her true feelings.

"What do you know about the local food bank?"

The question was so out of left field, Keisha couldn't process. "About what?"

"Food bank," Jack said impatiently.

"Ummm, they give out food to needy families." Keish wrinkled her brow. Maybe she wasn't getting fired. Phew.

"Yeah, yeah. Any idea on how the structure operates? Where they get their food from?"

"Sorry, boss." She'd never gone hungry. Thinking back on her childhood, she realized there were probably nights her mother had gone to bed starving because she'd always given food to Keisha and her brothers first.

"I need you to do a little undercover job for me." Jack stroked his index finger over the streak of scar tissue in his eyebrow.

Keisha scanned her knowledge of current disasters and couldn't come up with anything recent or high priority right now. And *nothing* that had to do with a food bank.

"Sure." Keisha rubbed her hands together. "Where'm I going?"

"Monterey County."

Right here at home?

Yeah, she got all the hotspots. But that was okay. She loved this job.

"Solo?" Because really, how dangerous could it be working a job for the food bank?

"Nope."

Hmm, maybe she'd get to work with Jess. That would be fun. Since they'd started going to lunch after the LeRoy mission, Jess had been working on Keisha to open up and hang out more, and somehow they had become friends. It was weird because Keisha didn't really have girlfriends. But Keisha liked it.

Before she could ask any more questions, someone knocked on the door, pounded really.

"Come on in," Jack yelled.

Keisha would have thought that having a live-in girlfriend would have mellowed out her very gruff boss but he still had the voice of a bull and no compunction about using it, loudly.

She turned around in the leather chair so she could see who had the heavy-handed fists.

And nearly swallowed her tongue as Shane Washington strolled through the door. He was a gorgeous hunk of man. Big, black, bald, and hot.

She'd been salivating over his superbly muscled physique and wicked smile since she started working for Jack months ago. And her initial physical attraction had exploded as she spent more time around him.

He was a total hottie on the outside and since she had the opportunity to work with him to save Maria Torres, she'd discovered what was inside was even hotter. His willingness to look out for those weaker than him was extremely appealing. In many ways he reminded her of Jack. But she didn't have any desire to jump Jack's bones.

The brother was built like a fricking Humvee. When he turned those striking dark chocolate eyes on her, Keisha wanted to melt into a steamy puddle of desire. Her lady parts tingled and her body perked up like he was a wide open fire hydrant on a hot summer day.

But of course, that wasn't her MO. Melting meant soft. And soft meant getting stepped all over. No. Fucking. Way.

So she got aggressive, pushed out of the leather chair, swaggered over to Shane, and then shoved out her hand. "Shane."

"Keisha." When his palm touched hers, her body jerked at the shock of sizzling attraction that bolted through her.

Day-am.

Shane blinked slow and easy, his lids drooped over his suddenly intense eyes and a deliberate, sexy smile spread over his face. He was sending out all the signals that he was attracted to her too. Even though he was a genuinely nice guy, he was also a player. A player who never seemed to settle on one woman.

And, she'd been burned by hope once before. She was still trying to get over her mortification from the last time they'd been in the same vicinity. A few months ago, when Shane had called her out of the blue and requested that she meet him, she'd hoped that he wanted to hook up with her.

So when she walked into that hotel room and saw Jack, Bliss, and Maria Torres, as well as Shane, her disappointment had been acute. Keisha needed to keep the memory of that disappointment front and center. Because that initial stab of reality in the face of her fantasy wishes had been painful.

Dumb, Keish. She'd set herself up for massive hurt.

Fortunately, no one had seemed to grasp she'd been disappointed when she'd realized that his call had been business, not personal.

Her mama had raised her to know that most people didn't stick and that hopes got you hurt. Keisha didn't need any more hurt in her life. So she dropped his hand and sank back down into the leather chair.

"Nice to see you again," Shane's deep voice rumbled from his chest. He always looked like he was on the verge of a laugh, his full lips tilted up slightly in the beginnings of a smirk.

Keisha bobbed her head in acknowledgement. But she didn't verbally reciprocate his sentiment since she'd hoped that she wouldn't see him again. She made it a firm policy never to lie in her personal life. Work was another story. Her work called for deception pretty damn often.

"Have a seat." Jack gestured to the unoccupied chair across from his desk. "I need your help."

Help? That seemed a little silly since he was her boss. And certainly didn't make sense if he was sending her on a job.

"What'cha got?" Keisha poised to take notes on her smart phone. Her actions helped her avoid Shane's inquisitive gaze. She wondered if she was flying somewhere since Shane was their on-call pilot. Except Jack had said the job was local.

When Jack didn't say anything, Keisha lifted her attention from the screen of her phone to look at her boss. He shifted his gaze between Keisha and Shane, who was uncharacteristically silent.

"Are you willing to go undercover?"

Jack knew she'd do whatever he needed her to do, so Keisha assumed Jack was asking Shane. She had a sudden premonition that she wasn't going to like whatever Jack said next.

With reluctant fascination, Keisha turned her regard to the large man next to her. And all over again she was struck by his size. Damn, he was big.

Shane's eyebrows rose, crinkling his forehead, and a wide smile graced his mouth. "Absolutely."

"Awesome."

Jack pulled a pair of tickets out of his suit pocket and held them up like cards. "I assume you have a suit?"

Shane grimaced. "Yeah."

Then Jack's intensity shifted to Keisha. "You got a formal dress or do you need the company credit card to go shopping?"

Keisha, normally pretty quick on the uptake, was having trouble processing. Her brain had gotten caught up as she pictured Shane in a suit.

"What—" she asked stupidly, "—do I need a formal dress for?"

"I need you two to go undercover." Jack waved the tickets at her. "At a charity wine event."

Undercover? Together? Oh, hell no, she did not need that. She was already way too fascinated with Shane Washington. The last thing she needed was to spend more time in his company. But she couldn't say no. Not to her boss. She had no valid reason to turn the job down.

Shane tried to stop the snicker that escaped but it was too late. The look on Keisha Johnson's face was priceless. She wanted to say no, but she wouldn't because Jack was her boss. He had to wonder if she wanted to say no because it meant spending more time with him, or if there was another reason. He didn't like the idea that she didn't want to work with him. But he loved seeing her riled up. Ever since that op last November she would pop into his thoughts at random times and he'd wonder what drove her.

Keisha snapped her mouth shut and glared at him.

Shane cleared his throat. He knew when to pull out an apology and this was definitely the time. "Sorry."

Way to get off on the wrong foot, Washington.

And, shit he should not be thinking about getting off while he was sitting next to the hottest woman of his acquaintance. He'd always thought she was gorgeous. Her curves had curves and she had an ass that he'd love to dig his hands into.

But what really did it for him was her attitude and smarts. A killer combination. But she worked for Jack, and in business Shane stuck to a 'no frat' policy. Leftover regs from his days in the military.

But damn, she was fine.

And he wasn't going to lie, he'd occasionally fantasized about her while he'd been alone. With his dick in his hand and a massive erection.

Of course, after he laughed, she wasn't going to get with him. Especially not if she thought he was laughing at her. But now was not the time to explain, so he returned to Jack's favor. "More of a beer guy, Jack."

"Not tonight you're not."

"It's Valentine's Day." Keisha ignored Shane, propped her fists on her hips, and tilted her head at Jack. "What if I have a date?"

Shane was fascinated by everything about her. She… shimmered. There was no other word for it. Her broad, flat cheekbones were dusted with some sort of bronze powder.

Her eyelids sparkled with a subtle gold shine that only enhanced her hazel eyes, and her dark mahogany hair was streaked with deep gold and auburn.

She was like a shimmering, shiny star and the urge to reach out and curl his fist around all that shiny was intense, overwhelming. Shane swallowed and shoved the desire way down inside. Business. No frat, he reminded himself reluctantly.

Jack blanched. "Geez, Keish, I didn't even think about that."

"Well if you want to keep that girl of yours you better think about it quick," she snarked back at him.

A goofy smile spread over Jack's face and his whole countenance shifted.

"Hey, I know." Keisha snapped her fingers, a bright yellow polish on her nails. "Why don't you take Bliss to a charity wine event?"

"Ha. Ha." Jack shoved the tickets at Shane.

Shane gripped the thick paper in his meaty fists. He wanted to know why Jack was sending them to a charity event. Somehow Shane didn't think Jack was playing matchmaker.

"What's the problem?" Shane asked.

"Someone's giving food to the food bank."

"Isn't that the point of the food bank?" Keisha's question sounded eager as she reached for a reason to turn this assignment down. "People donate and then it's distributed to those who need it?"

"Someone is depositing fresh produce in the warehouse after hours." Jack crossed his arms over his chest, his butt was on the edge of his desk, and his legs were extended straight, feet crossed at the ankles. "The problem is that the food hasn't been vetted and they have no idea where it came

from. I've got a lab testing the broccoli right now but the food bank can't distribute the food until we know for sure that it is safe and where it came from."

"So how and why are we undercover?" Shane couldn't get the image of Keisha under the covers out of his head. He leaned forward and bent slightly at the waist, so that his semi-hard cock wouldn't be visible to Jack or Keisha.

Jesus, he needed to stop thinking about her naked. Like, now.

"Here's your cover." Jack pointed at them, his face serious. "The Washingtons are considering a sizable donation to the food bank but before they fork over the money they want to check out the facility and the way the organization is run. They are very hands on philanthropists."

"A wine event." Keisha snorted and her head rocked a little. "Stupid. Wouldn't it be better to have the philanthropists actually donate food?"

"They have several fundraisers a year where they wine and dine the local population and then they convince them to open their checkbooks." Jack frowned. "Food for Life is a particular favorite of my mom's. And The Stone Foundation contributes a fair amount every year."

"I still don't understand why we have to go undercover as a couple." Keisha pursed her mouth, her bronze lip gloss gleamed in the early morning light of Jack's office. Shane forced his attention away from her luscious mouth. "Why can't you just investigate?"

"We'll actually be there too." Jack said, "The chairman asked me as a favor to get to the bottom of what is going on. But the board knows me and my brothers and my sister. It's clearly an inside job in some way. So...I needed to bring in someone they don't know."

Shane listened to Jack babble on about times and locations and other logistics for tonight's 'mission', but he was still stuck back on one heart-pounding, libido-inciting, temperature-raising fact.

Hells yeah. They were going to be a couple.

CHAPTER 2

Keisha checked her silhouette in the mirror. She'd bought the slinky black cocktail dress for a trip to Las Vegas with her old boyfriend. But he'd bailed at the last minute.

She looked damned fine in the tight, short dress. Her red lace, push up bra created cleavage that gave her interesting shadows in the keyhole cutout, and the little bit of spandex in the dress caused it to cling to her well-apportioned ass. While she always thought she was a little too round, guys had yet to complain about the size of her butt.

And what the hell was she doing thinking about her assets in this dress? Her heart beat in triple time against her ribcage as she thought about the upcoming assignment. Tonight was just to lay the groundwork. She and Shane were supposed to go and cement their cover as a wealthy, philanthropic couple looking for a new cause to support.

The plan was to get an invite to visit the actual warehouse, hopefully tomorrow, and check out the security and see if they could set up a place for surveillance so they could catch whoever was covertly delivering the produce in the act.

She was one part excited about spending time with Shane, and one part annoyed with herself for being excited about spending time with Shane. But she couldn't deny that just being in the same space as the hot, big man raised her awareness of both him and her own body.

Her nipples tightened and her sex tingled as she thought about having to pretend to be Shane's wife. He was going to have to touch her. Of course, it wouldn't be anything too intimate but she was going to have to steel herself for the feel of his rough, callused hands against her skin.

She slipped her feet into the four inch heels with gladiator straps and a zipper up the back and admired the sleek shimmer of the body lotion on her legs and arms. The light spicy fragrance enveloped her and gave her confidence a much needed boost.

Shane Washington was a player.

She knew it. And she needed to keep that fact front and center in her mind.

A heavy pounding startled her out of her thoughts. She'd wanted to meet Shane at the restaurant where the event was being held, but he'd argued that they were a couple and would logically drive together. She'd relented but she hated the idea of having Shane in her home, fearing once he'd been in her space, she and it would never be the same.

Shane Washington banged on the door of the nondescript condo. He was pumped about this small assignment for several reasons. One, he'd been restless lately. A little action was welcome. Two, he was looking forward to spending time with Keisha Johnson. Usually he avoided any kind of interaction with women he worked with. Besides the fact that the no fraternization policy pretty much worked, he tried to keep things with women light and easy. He wasn't a long term prospect and he had no wish to piss off people, women especially, that he worked with. But ever since last November, Keisha Johnson had been on his mind.

A strange exhilaration gripped him. He couldn't wait to spend time with her. The rush of adrenaline and thrill of anticipation was the same as when he was about to lift off the runway. And he began sporting wood at the thought. Fantastic. She was going to answer the door and see his hard on.

All his life, all he'd ever wanted to do was fly. Nothing had even come close to the high he got from being thousands of feet in the air. But standing on Keisha Johnson's front porch had just come a close second.

She yanked the door open and Shane couldn't say a word.

Her curves were amply displayed in a skintight black dress. The neckline of the dress was a wide band of shiny gold and circled her neck demurely, but then her dress had some sort of cut out that showed her cleavage, revealing the mounds of her breasts and enticing shadows that he wanted to explore with his tongue. He was almost desperate to see if she tasted as good as she looked. The dip in her waist was tiny compared to her gorgeous breasts and her fantastically grabbable hips.

Shane could imagine her on top of him riding him like a freaking bronco as he gripped her hips and pounded up into her. Suddenly his heart was racing and sweat blossomed on his face. God damn, he wanted her.

Wanted to explore every lush inch of her Nubian body. Wanted to bury his cock in her hot slick pussy. Wanted to explode into the tight clench of her sex as she orgasmed around his cock.

She propped her fist on her hip and tilted her head.

Shane cleared his throat. "You look fantastic."

"Let's go."

"We can't yet. We need to get comfortable with each other." He knew they needed to practice touching each other in a non-sexual way. He definitely needed some pre-work if just looking at her caused his body to react so intensely.

"What are you talking about?" She was all tough attitude and snark. But he'd seen the softer side of Keisha when they'd protected Maria Torres a few months ago. That had been an eye-opener. And ever since he'd seen that inner marshmallow, she'd been on his mind. He couldn't get her sweet side out of his head.

"We're supposed to be a married couple." Shane's body reacted again. And he wanted to touch her the way he'd been obsessing about for the last two months. But instead, a tame, informal hand on her face was all he could allow himself. Shane slowly brought his palm up to cup her cheek. Even with his cautious movement, she flinched when their skin touched.

"See," Shane said unnecessarily.

She shoved his forearm away from her body. But she didn't step back. Didn't make a move to put more distance between them. "That means nothing."

Shane leaned nearer, their bodies so close, their chests were almost touching. The scent of patchouli and lemon wafted from her heated skin. As he looked into her striking eyes, hazel swirled with gold, he saw her answering response to him.

Her eyes were brighter, her lungs expanded and

contracted faster, and her nipples had sharpened to points. If he took a deep breath, his pecs would make contact with her breasts.

Her mouth was slicked with siren red and her tongue peeked out to wet her lips.

Shane groaned. How could he resist that unconscious invitation?

He dipped his head, stared into her wide startled gaze, giving her plenty of time to avoid what was coming. But she didn't move. Didn't breathe if her absolute stillness was any indication.

"This is a monumentally bad idea," she whispered against the slow, soft brush of his lips.

"Hell no." He pressed a chaste kiss against the corner of her mouth, swiped his tongue against the seam of her lips, then nipped with his teeth, softly demanding entrance. "Best. Idea. Ever."

And then he kissed her. Really kissed her. Fully engaged, lips, tongue, teeth, devouring her mouth as if he'd die if he didn't taste her.

Keisha melted.

There was no other word for it. She sank against his larger, harder body. Her fingers lightly clasped his biceps and she tilted her head to give him better access. His cock brushed her slightly-rounded belly between her hipbones, and they both moaned.

Slow, slow, slow. He gently held her hips and rubbed against her. He could feel the hard contraction of her womb as her stomach tightened against his cock. Her response was uninhibited, genuine, and sexy as hell.

Keisha slid her hands up his muscled arms until her palms rested on his shoulders. He shivered at the sensual stroke of her fingers against the back of his neck.

His cock swelled. Shane whirled them around and pushed her up against the wall next to her front door.

Keisha was sandwiched between the hard press of his thick muscular chest and the unforgiving wall behind her. With her shoes on she was tall enough that the sculpted planes of his pecs rubbed sensuously over her stiff nipples.

Somnolent, sultry heat rose between them as he leaned closer and rubbed his nose along the surprisingly sensitive curve of her ear. His body dwarfed hers, his beefy thigh was wedged between her legs. A curious dizziness assailed her and Keisha swayed toward the magnetic draw of his sex appeal.

Keisha shivered.

Shane lifted her up and she whimpered. Holy shit. She was a solidly built woman and he'd lifted her up as if she were a stick thin model. He scraped his tongue down the side of her throat and nipped at the rounded curve of her shoulder. Then he opened his mouth over her neck and suckled.

His bulk towered over her, surrounding Keisha in a sexual haze. Her dress was tight enough that she couldn't wrap her legs around his waist. But then Shane cupped her ass in his large palms, and rubbed the ridge of her pubis against the pole in his pants. She moaned again as the slight friction stimulated her clit.

"Shit woman. You're like A-1 jet fuel at flashpoint." Shane let her down easily until the tips of her shoes touched the floor. He rested his head against the wall over her shoulder, his chest heaving and his fingers trembling as he smoothed his palm over the curve of her hip.

Keisha knew she needed to put her armor back in place. Put up that wall that kept people at a distance and protected her from heartbreak. In a second.

Right now she just savored him. It had been far longer than she'd like to admit since she'd had a man. And she'd never had anyone as masculine or as sheerly dominating as Shane. She could admit, if only just to herself, that he made her totally weak in the knees.

She'd combusted in his arms. Probably like every other woman he'd had.

Player, she reminded herself. She needed to subdue her yearning, and get them back on track and out the door.

"Quit wasting time." She dismissed the earthquake worthy kiss as nothing more than a platonic peck on the cheek. "We met. We got married. We want to give money to a worthy cause. The end."

CHAPTER 3

Shane nearly swallowed his tongue as Keisha sauntered toward the restaurant, her hips swinging provocatively. All he could do was follow behind her.

He'd been infatuated with Keisha over the last few months, and he figured he'd exaggerated her sex appeal in his mind. But after that amazing, intense kiss in her entryway, he acknowledged he'd been way off fucking base.

She was hot.

Scorching, crazy hot. And their kiss had been even hotter. If he hadn't promised Jack he would investigate this problem for the food bank, Shane would have stripped off her sexy dress and taken her against the wall.

Now he watched hungrily as she entered the wine and dine event like she owned it. The small restaurant had exposed brick walls, a thick-beamed ceiling, rustic copper accents, and a large flagstone fireplace. The hearth was decorated with red hearts and wine bottles tied with white and red bows.

Shane hustled up behind her and placed his palm on her bare shoulder. "Hold up, babe." His voice was even lower than normal as he suppressed the desire to run his hand over her smooth, soft skin.

She turned her head and gave him a 'cold as a glacier ice cap' smile while her eyes shot sparks that told him he'd pushed the intimate touch just a little too far. Her curls brushed her shoulder and the curve of her neck. Shane's eyes widened when he saw the faint mark from his kiss. Holy hell, he'd given her a hickey.

"Uh, Keish."

Before he could confess, a well-preserved white woman approached them. She was in her early sixties with a cap of silver hair that curled around her face, blue eyes that sparkled as brightly as the giant diamonds in her ears, and dressed in a traditional suit in a pale purple.

"Welcome to the Food for Life fundraiser," she extended her right hand to Keisha and smiled eagerly.

"Keisha Washington." The slight rasp of Keisha's voice scraped over his nerve endings, and all Shane could think about was listening to that husky rasp while he thrust inside her. "And this is my husband," Keisha stumbled over the intimate word, "Shane."

"I'm Monica Peterson, on the board at Food for Life. It's a pleasure to meet both of you." Monica said, "Can I get you a glass of wine?"

"None for me." Shane passed. He was driving.

"I'd love one."

"Great. Come with me and I'll tell you all about our organization."

Keisha tried to make it look like she was sorry to be deserting Shane but he caught the glee in her hazel gaze as she tried to stay in character as a loving, adoring wife. He was pretty sure she pulled it off, unless you looked closely, you couldn't see the edge in her eyes. "You going to be okay?"

"Babe. Enjoy yourself." He brushed his knuckles along her cheekbone and then kissed her forehead. And damn, she smelled good. What started as a teasing gesture, turned into something more as he inhaled her unique scent.

Shane knew he was going to pay for that touch later. So he might as well go all the way. He smiled indulgently and put his hand on her butt and pushed gently.

Her gaze narrowed. "Oh, believe me, I will." Her natural sass shone through the words.

Shane grinned. "You do that."

While Monica Peterson lead Keisha toward a bar set up in the far corner, Shane glanced around the restaurant. They were closed to the public. Some of the tables had been removed leaving a large open area in the center of the room. Couples mingled in groups of mostly two and four. Waiters in black pants, white shirts, and black bow ties served mini-sliders and crab cakes on silver platters. He headed toward the bar, in the opposite direction of the one that Keisha had taken, to get a glass of water. Before he could take more than a few steps, a man with a name tag that identified him as Bob Michaels, the Chair of the Food for Life Board of Directors, intercepted him. "Mr. Washington?"

Shane raised his eyebrows. "Yes." He wasn't sure if he should be offended by the assumption that he was Shane Washington, but when he'd taken in the fairly small crowd, there were very few black men in the room.

"Jack told me you were built like a linebacker with the smile of a little kid." He stuck out his hand to shake Shane's.

"Jack's gonna get his ass kicked." But Shane laughed.

Jack came up behind Shane. "Not if I kick yours first."

Of course, Shane'd known Jack was going to be there. That was part of the cover. Jack was introducing Shane and Keisha to the food bank opportunity.

"Nice to meet you." Bob Michaels leaned closer. "If you have any specific questions, let me know."

More attendees entered the circle surrounding Shane, Jack, and Bob Michaels and welcomed him to the Food for Life wine and dine. The press of people made him slightly uncomfortable. He preferred not to be the center of attention. He was more of a behind-the-scenes kind of guy. It came from his days growing up where drawing attention to yourself was the last thing an African-American kid in his neighborhood needed to be doing.

Keisha pretended to wander back toward Shane but if anyone had been paying particular attention, they would have seen that she made it to his side in record time. The older man talking to Shane seemed innocuous enough but she recognized the tension in Shane's shoulders. What surprised her even more was her intuitiveness about Shane. She wasn't even sure how she knew to read his body language. It was definitely subtle but she'd identified his unease immediately. How? She had no idea.

Keisha wondered what caused his tension and set off her worry meter. Shane could handle himself and this assignment was far from dangerous, so why was he tense?

She stepped up to the cluster of people just as the older man declared, "Mr. Washington is considering a sizable donation to our organization, but only after he observes how we run our business."

"My wife and I would like to hear more about your operation," Shane said. He wrapped his arm lightly around her waist, and she was thankful for the fact that he had made them practice touching. Otherwise she'd have likely shot through the roof at the arc of electricity that zipped up her spine.

Shane inclined his head. She placed a manicured hand on his forearm. The muscled strength beneath her fingers caused a flutter of weakness through her limbs.

Day-am, even his forearms were ripped.

She had a totally inappropriate mind scatter, as she imagined for a moment, what Shane would look like without his shirt on.

"Don Wallaston." A pompous husky gentleman in a bowtie with a mane of white hair combed artlessly away from his red face shoved out his hand. "What's your business?"

"Washington Aviation," Shane replied, his voice a mere rumble as he shook the older man's hand.

"Your thirty thousand dollars would be put to very good use." Another older woman dripping in diamonds, with a wrinkled neck that didn't match her too smooth face, a little too much Botox perhaps, smiled and leaned into Shane's arm after introducing herself as Jane Pavlov.

Keisha fought the urge to growl. She did not like that woman's hand on her man's body. Anywhere.

Oh, good God, Shane was not *her* man.

But then their words registered. Thirty thousand dollars. Maybe that's what Shane was tense about. Besides the chairman who asked Stone Consulting to look into the strange clandestine deliveries, everyone else thought Shane and Keisha would be donating a cool 30K to the food bank.

"And this is Keisha, Shane's lovely wife." Jack laid it on a little too thick in Keisha's opinion.

Damn Jack for not thinking this through. Keisha would make sure that the Stone family ponied up the money. She gave Jack a death stare. She hated having to subdue her acerbic personality.

Don, the older dude, leered at Keisha, his laser focus on her neck. "Are you newlyweds?"

Shane slid his palm up her arm and circled her shoulders. His thick bulky bicep felt fantastic against her back. She tilted her head on Shane's arm and smiled at the old man. "Fairly newlywed." As in this morning. Not that it was any of his business and Keisha fought the urge to say that.

Another man smirked, and the older woman who'd been subtly coming on to Shane, frowned at Keisha.

Shane tensed again. Poor guy.

"Practically still on our honeymoon." He nuzzled her ear and whispered, "Sorry."

It was Keisha's turn to stiffen. What the heck was he talking about? But then their embrace in her doorway flashed in her mind, the tight, hard suction of his gorgeous lips against her neck.

Hickey, Jack mouthed at Keisha, confirming her suspicions.

She narrowed her eyes at Shane, her temper flashing. "You didn't?" she hissed.

He pressed a gentle kiss against the side of her head and then murmured in her ear, "Babe, it was an accident."

And if they'd been any place else, she would have let him have it. But she couldn't let go of the tight rein on her temper, because when she went off, she could forget everything and she couldn't blow their cover. But she mentally promised retaliation when the night ended.

She looked forward to giving him sharp edge of her tongue. But instead of yelling at him, another use for her tongue invaded her brain, the vision of her licking up and down his thick, hard cock had her knees weakening and a rush of arousal flooding her sex.

Accident, her ass. "You're in for it now."

But Shane only smiled, his lips lifted in a wicked smirk. "Lookin' forward to it."

"And there goes my girlfriend, Bliss." Jack had a ridiculously goofy look on his face as he stared after his new girlfriend, Bliss Lee. She was half-Irish, half-Chinese and absolutely gorgeous. Keisha had never seen her boss and friend so whipped and she'd known him a long time.

Keisha had met Jack when they were both in Basic at the Great Lakes Naval Training Center in Michigan. Apparently he and Bliss had a thing before he went into the Navy. Then they reconnected on a case a few months ago.

Jack took off toward Bliss. He needed to run interference. Part of the plan was for Bliss to keep Shelley, Jack's stepmother, away from Shane and Keisha. Jack had to make sure that his stepmother didn't see them at the fundraiser because Shelley knew Keisha from the company and Shane from their charter flights. Since Shelley knew that Keisha and Shane were not together, let alone married, they didn't want Shelley to accidentally out them.

"Behave yourself." Jack aimed a stern look at Keisha before he beelined for his girlfriend.

Bob Michaels cleared his throat. "So, Mr. Washington—"

"Call me Shane." Shane slowly took his attention from Keisha, making it clear he was doing so on his own terms. And he didn't let go of her but held her tightly against him.

"What would you like to know about Food for Life?"

"Take me through your donation and distribution process," Shane demanded authoritatively.

For the next ten minutes, Bob Michaels gave a

rudimentary overview of the processes involved in collecting donations, sorting, boxing, and distributing food. The other attendees filled in details.

"We don't actually distribute to individuals." Jane, the diamond dripping woman added, "We distribute the food to our partners, food kitchens, churches, after school programs, the county. They hand out the food packages, or actual cooked food, to the individuals in need."

Keisha had never really thought about the logistics of feeding a transient community.

"What about fresh produce?" Keisha stood up straighter. And for a moment, she wasn't thinking about the job but about the kids. "We've got to teach our kids that fruits and vegetables are essential to good health."

"Great question." The older woman's smile warmed as she expounded on a subject that was clearly one of her favorites. "We get donations from a variety of sources. We are working to put in place a program where donors can sponsor an acre of land and we employ the workers to plant, care and harvest food directly for us."

Bob Michaels eagerly interjected. "We also have a healthy gleaning program, where people who have produce trees and vines in their yards allow us to come in and harvest fruit when it is ripe."

"Are there any regulations on produce donations?" Keisha wondered since the reason they needed to investigate was because someone was giving large donations anonymously.

"Not really." Don Wallaston shook his head.

So why would someone donate food anonymously? There wasn't any point to it and they would lose the tax benefit. Right? But she pretended that all that information wasn't swirling around in her head.

"That's fantastic." Keisha's mouth curved into a wide smile.

Shane's chest was nearly pressed up against her back as Shane wrapped a thick arm around her waist. His embrace was more intoxicating than the mellow, fruity merlot she'd gulped down in a bid to calm her nerves. She'd been rock solid when she'd tried to illegally scam her way in to Henri LeRoy's mansion in Port-du-Bois…and if she'd been discovered trying to plant poison there, she'd have been dead. Here she'd just be asked to leave. So why was she nervous?

This assignment was practically a boondoggle. Dress up. Eat fancy food. Drink excellent wine. The good news was that she had enough experience to act as if she belonged in this room with all these wealthy people.

Keisha could throw attitude with the best of them, so she sucked it up and pretended that she had the money and the right to be a legitimate guest at this party rather than a fake who'd grown up one step away from needing the services of the food bank.

Shane asked some more questions. "Do the recipients have to be homeless?" He was unbelievably tense behind her. "There are plenty of single mothers out there who work two jobs to put a roof over their kids' heads and food on the table."

"Not at all," Monica replied. "Many of the county's recipients are working families who are struggling to pay their bills and rent. There is a misconception that the food bank only supplies to the homeless, when that couldn't be further from the truth."

Keisha had almost forgotten that they were there to garner an invite to the facility, but she was reminded when

Monica Peterson said, "Why don't you come over to the warehouse tomorrow and we'll show you around."

"Sounds good," Shane's voice rumbled from behind her, the deep sound vibrated through her. "Would it be possible to actually work in the warehouse tomorrow?"

"Of course!" Don Wallaston's smile threatened to split the man's face in two. Keisha could practically see the dollar signs in his pupils, like the old cartoons she used to watch while her momma cleaned houses on Saturday mornings.

They made plans to go to the warehouse tomorrow morning. The board members were clearly anxious for the influx of cash. And they would have kept them there for another hour but Keisha saw Bliss Lee signal them. They needed to leave. It was clear that Jack wasn't going to be able to keep Shelley corralled in the other room of the restaurant. So Shane and Keisha bid hasty goodbyes with the board waved enthusiastically as Shane and Keisha left.

They sauntered toward Shane's red Charger. Keisha tried to tug her fingers from his, but Shane held tight to her hand. "Got to keep up appearances," he argued.

On the way back to Keisha's condo, they kept the conversation on logistics for tomorrow and how they would approach scoping out the warehouse facility.

They finally arrived back at Keisha's condo. "Thanks for the ride. See you tomorrow."

She curled her fingers around the door handle, but before she could make her escape, Shane exited the car and had come around to the passenger door. He opened the door for her and held out his palm to help her gracefully exit the bucket seat.

"Um, there's one last thing." Shane shifted uncomfortably in front of her but he hadn't let go of her hand.

Keisha tugged discretely. "What?"

She couldn't imagine why he looked so discomfited. He took a deep breath, squared his shoulders. "I really did want to say I'm sorry."

She'd actually forgotten. But now the memory of the old guy leering at her came back. "A hickey? Really?"

"You're a potent woman."

She couldn't help the little thrill that zoomed through her at his words. What would it be like to make Shane Washington lose total control?

She snorted. "Not that potent."

At her derisive words, he crowded her against the side of the car, his muscular bulk blocked out her view of the parking lot and everyone else. "Very. Potent." His voice was low and tight.

And just like that, her brain went straight to the picture of her sucking another part of his anatomy. He was one fine man.

Keisha's eyelids drooped, and her tongue swept over lips just thinking about discovering Shane Washington's naked secrets.

He groaned low and deep in his throat. "What are you thinking about?"

Her gaze dropped the large bulge in his pants. "Breaking rules."

Jesus, the blatant lust in Keisha's gaze slayed him. Shane's cock swelled, growing even harder and all he could think about was him and her and how hot it would be.

"Fuck." Shane swiveled his hips so that his erection brushed her body. "Right there with you."

He bent to capture her mouth with his, then pulled her bottom lip and suckled lightly. Fuck he wanted to be inside her. "Invite me in," he demanded huskily. Screw his no fraternization rule.

Keisha Johnson hit all his sexual buttons. She was more than a handful both physically and attitude-wise. She didn't back down and gave better than she got. He wanted all that fire and sass in his arms, in his bed.

"Convince me," she shot back.

"I want you. I want to see you naked. Suck on your nipples. Finger your clit and drive you wild. I want your fingernails digging into my skin as I go down on you. I want to fuck you until we're both sweaty and sated and trembling from the force of how hard we come."

She whimpered, and he was pretty sure he had her.

But he wasn't above begging. "I ache for you. Put me out of my misery. You won't regret it."

CHAPTER 4

Keisha knew this was a bad idea. But damn, he was fine. And he set her body on fire with just a few words and the hot suction of his mouth.

Shane said, "Please."

What really did it for her was the fact that what should have been begging was uttered as a demand. A gush of arousal flooded her pussy. She'd been lusting after him since she'd first laid eyes on Shane. And here he was, at her front door. Locked and loaded.

"Inside," she commanded. "Now." She whirled around and headed for her condo.

Shane fell back a little and she knew he was checking her out. Keisha put a little extra sway in her step and was rewarded when he said breathlessly, "Damn, babe."

She hastily unlocked the door and pushed inside. She wanted him. And now that she'd made the decision…she needed to get to a bed, before she changed her mind, came to her clouded senses, and concluded this was an epically bad decision.

She stalked inside with a sultry swing of her hips and listened triumphantly as his breath caught in his throat.

His elegant, exquisitely-fitted suit and the very stuffy tie really did it for her. All that ripped muscle packaged in such proper attire made her want to unwrap him like a kid tearing open her present on Christmas morning. Keisha twirled and tugged at the formal tie around Shane's neck. The action hauled him closer, and the heat pouring off his body was incendiary.

He bent his head and dragged his tongue from the top of the keyhole down into the valley of her breasts. He wasn't touching her anywhere else and the wet heat was unbelievably erotic. Then he dropped to his knees and nuzzled her breasts even as he slid his palms up the backs of her thighs.

Shane marveled at her smooth skin as he pushed her short dress up her legs until his palms met the bare skin of her ass. Keisha clutched his head against her breasts and rocked her pelvis into his abs.

He traced her thong down until his fingers delved beneath the fragile lace and stroked the swollen lips of her sex. Shane sucked in a breath. "God damn, you're soaking wet."

He slid the tip of his middle finger inside her slick channel, just lightly penetrating her.

Shane looked up at her. Her head was tilted back in abandon. But her fingers were working at the buttons on his shirt, nearly frantic as if she'd die if she didn't touch his bare skin.

Shane pushed her dress up until it bunched beneath her breasts and bared her stomach and the red lace thong to his gaze. "Hot damn, that is gorgeous."

"Happy Valentine's Day," she said breathlessly.

"Thank God for St. Valentine." He kissed a path from her belly button down to the waist of her underwear, all the while his middle finger pumped in and out of her sex. Her scent was driving him crazy.

Musky wetness coated his finger and slicked her pussy lips as she rocked harder into his hand. Shane tongued her clit then sucked the bud into his mouth. She moaned long and loud.

"Fuck me," she groaned.

"You going to be a loud lover, babe?" Fuck, he wanted her screaming.

"If you're good enough," she sassed right back at him.

Damn, his cock pulsed against the zipper of his fancy black pants. Shane needed to relieve the pressure. He slid his fingers out of her pussy. She rocked closer to him.

"Minute." He ripped the zipper down and unbuttoned his pants until his cock sprang free from the confines of the black silk.

"Turn around," he said gutturally.

She hesitated. But then she obeyed the command. Shane unzipped her dress, unhooked her bra, and pushed everything off her shoulders and down her body. Her butt was round and plump and he couldn't resist the primal urge to nip at her generous curves as he shoved the thong to the floor.

"No way we're making it to a bed the first time," he growled.

Keisha's knees dipped. Her dress and underwear pooled at her feet. Shane had never seen a more erotic sight as she waited for him ceding control in this moment.

He directed her. "Bend over the arm of the sofa."

She didn't even hesitate this time. She took two long strides and bent over. She turned and looked over her

shoulder and smiled wickedly. As if daring him to come and get it.

Keisha had never been more turned on in her life.

Thick liquid coated the inside of her thighs and she was empty, desolate. "I need you inside me. Now."

As he pushed to his feet, Shane's cock bobbed from the nest of curls at his groin. He was huge. Not a complete surprise since he was a very large man. His long, thick staff stretched toward the ceiling, his erection as dark as the rest of him except for the deep red, engorged head.

"Oh my god." Her knees threatened to buckle at the thought of all that delicious man inside her.

"Just call me Shane," he teased as he shoved his pants off and strode over to her. His cock bobbed against the flat rippling muscles of his lower abdomen. He still wore the suit jacket and his shirt hung open playing peek a boo with his extremely ripped abs.

"Damn, babe, you are gorgeous." He smoothed his palm over her round butt and her entire body reacted to the subtle caress. Her pussy tingled and her nipples tightened into even harder points. Shit, she needed him inside her now. His rubbed his fingers along her slit and spread her juices over her pussy. "So fucking wet."

Shane took his hand away and pumped his cock once.

Keisha whimpered at the sight.

Shane thanked God that he'd had the forethought to put a condom in his suit jacket. More hopeful than premeditated, but hope was a powerful emotion.

He snatched the little packet from the interior pocket as he shrugged the jacket off, then rolled the protection over his cock. He couldn't remember the last time he'd been this hard. Keisha had spread her legs, arched her back, just waiting for him. Her pussy was flushed a deep dark rose, lips swollen and plumped, peeking through her mahogany curls. Just waiting for him to slam home.

"You want me, babe?"

Shane was a talker. He liked to tell his lover exactly what he was going to do. He knew from his former lovers that he was big so he tried to prepare them with words before he actually penetrated them.

"Now," she snarled. "Hard. Fast."

"Can't." He brushed the head of his cock against her slit, her juices coated the condom, and a slick heat poured from her body. She was so freaking hot.

"Got to take it slow." Shane pressed just the head inside her and paused. "Too big otherwise."

Keisha tried to push back against him to impale herself on his dick. But Shane held her hips, and forced himself to proceed gently.

With one long, agonizingly slow glide, he buried himself to the hilt in her heat.

He groaned. His balls snugged up tight against her swollen sex, and her slick channel pulsed around him, eagerly trying to strangle his cock.

"Move, dammit."

Shane started a slow back and forth, rocking his hips into hers and savoring that moment when he was completely surrounded by her wet heat. The slow pace was killing him but he didn't want to hurt her.

"Harder," she sobbed.

He controlled the pace of his thrusts, trying to make it last as long as possible and to let her body accommodate to the intrusion of his cock. But Keisha was having none of that. She rose onto her tiptoes and with one hard shift of her hips, she slammed back against him. Her ass hit his abdomen so hard she almost pushed him back a step. But the sensation of him fully seated in her tight pussy was too much. "Harder," she demanded again.

Shane groaned and gave in to her demands. "I'm going to pound into you now. I'll hit your g-spot so hard that you'll see stars, and your sweet pussy will tighten around me."

Keisha moaned again. "Just do it already."

And Shane let loose. He gripped her hips and shoved his cock hard, she spread her legs wider to give him room to move. And he began a steady, brutal pace until Keisha came with a keening cry.

Her back arched, she threw her head back, every muscle in her body tightened even as her sex constricted around his cock in intense hard pulls and sucked his orgasm from his body in violent clenches.

Shane roared as he came. He pumped into her, his head went light and his heart boomed in his chest. A sense of absolute perfection overcame him. Sweat slicked his skin as his cock emptied, and his mind emptied of everything, except her.

He still had his shirt on. Keisha was naked but for the black gladiator heels, which was totally hot. Her skin glimmered in the soft light from the lamp beside the sofa. His thighs were like jelly and her legs quivered right along with his.

He was wrecked.

And he didn't want to withdraw from her body. To lose the physical connection that bound them.

But then concern and remorse eddied through him. He'd taken her like an animal, mounted her from behind, without asking if she was comfortable like that. Behaved like a freaking caveman.

He wrapped his arms around her waist, still buried inside her sex and rested his cheek against her spine. He pressed a soft kiss, even though it was too late for softness, against her ridiculously supple skin.

"You okay?" he asked, and waited for her to rip him a new one. He was usually so careful to protect and care for the woman he was with because he was a big guy. He hadn't wanted to hurt her. But damn, he'd lost total control.

She laughed huskily. The reverberations rippled through his chest and along his cock. "Better than okay," she purred. "Give me a few minutes and we can move to the bed for round two."

"I didn't hurt you?"

"Hell no, Shane." She slid her fingers between his and gripped his hand in hers.

"I was worried that I was too hard," he confessed. He didn't think it was the time to mention that some of his previous lovers had trouble with his…enthusiasm.

Keisha pushed to standing, her back pressed against his chest, and her ass snugged against his lower abdomen, and his already semi-hard again cock slipped from her slick channel.

She turned around and launched herself at him, wrapping her legs around his waist, and climbing his body. "Do it again."

CHAPTER 5

Keisha lay still and absorbed the quiet morning. The scent of them, the musk of sex, and the soft lemon from the candle on her bedside table permeated the sheets and invaded her senses. The air was the slightest bit chilly, their bodies covered only by the soft cotton sheet.

They had destroyed her bed. Her bold geometric print comforter and the jewel-hued throw pillows had been shoved to the floor as they'd rolled around. Memories bombarded her. Shane, hard and heavy between her spread thighs, conquering her body. Keisha riding him shamelessly, his hands rough and insistent as he played with her breasts. Keisha taking his gorgeous cock into her mouth, caressing his balls, and sucking him dry.

The images were turning her on again. Shane had insinuated the hard column of his thigh between her legs, and her butt was snuggled against his rapidly growing erection.

Early morning light filtered in through her sheer curtains. She'd forgotten to close her drapes last night. She'd had…other things on her mind, on *her*. She repressed the urge to giggle.

Her, giggle. Seriously, she hadn't felt this light in a very long time.

Shane's heat warmed the bed and her body as she thought about his contradictions.

She'd seen him be extremely menacing. And yet, sometimes, he imparted such a serene air. That dichotomy was unbelievably appealing.

He was exactly who he was and was entirely at peace with himself. His tranquility wormed into her consciousness, and she wondered if she could just be here with him, calm, peaceful. Just be.

When she was with Shane, the chaos in her head quieted and the need to protect herself faded into the background. Which was dangerous. She couldn't depend on him. She couldn't depend on anyone but herself. Her momma had raised her to know that people didn't stick so you couldn't lean on anyone. Wasn't that true of her daddy?

He hadn't even stayed around until she was born.

And that quickly, the serenity and lightness disappeared. Shane Washington was a player. She'd been foolish to jump into bed with him, even as world-rocking as the sex had been. The aftermath was likely going to suck.

Shane trailed his finger along the curve of her neck and heaved a sigh. "What are you worrying about in there?" He pressed his lips along the same path his finger had taken.

"The job."

Shane snorted. "No way. You can handle anything that's thrown at you for work without batting an eyelash. Those tense muscles are personal."

Keisha didn't know whether to cringe or preen at the

fact that he apparently knew her well enough to realize that she was fearless when it came to work.

She wasn't about to admit that she'd been thinking about him. About what a delicious mistake having sex with him was.

"I can see that chip growing like a cloud in a thunderstorm."

Keisha glanced at the clock on the bedside table. "We need to get to the food bank." She ignored his queries.

Shane sighed again.

"I've got a change of clothes in my trunk." He pressed a kiss on her ear.

Figured. Player.

"I keep a Go Bag packed in case my clients need me for an emergency," he clarified.

"I'm sure that comes in handy." For when he scores with some chick stupid enough to fall into bed with him.
Like her.

It was pretty hard to miss the sarcasm in her voice.

"Yeah. It does." Shane pushed out of the bed. "I'm going to take a shower."

He stood beside the bed. His body ripped with muscle, his chest broad, his cock half erect and weeping with a few drops of pre-come. And if she'd been standing, she'd have had to brace herself. He seriously made her knees weak.

Keisha was nuts. She had a hot man in her house. Naked and half-primed. One who had seriously rocked her world last night. The best sex she'd had in a very long time. Maybe ever. And today they were going to pretend to be married. She needed to forget about shutting down her emotions, forget about that future hurt that was surely on the way, and enjoy him.

She grabbed a condom from the bedside table. "Want company?"

KEISHA AND SHANE spent the day working at the warehouse, learning about the way donations came in, how they were sorted, and then re-boxed to distribute to the food bank's clients. They toured the enormous refrigerated room and she'd been surprised by the amount of fresh produce and fruit that was donated and then given away. Even more interesting, the numbers of families the food bank fed on a monthly basis was pretty staggering.

Keisha left the warehouse grateful for her mother's sacrifice and yet, thankful that nowadays struggling families had access to help if they needed it. Shane had been a thoughtful and industrious volunteer worker, asking questions that showed he also had grown up in a household where money and food had been tight.

Hours later, Shane and Keisha were back at the warehouse, after hours and undercover. Jack had given them a key and the information on how to avoid the security cameras.

They were set up on the catwalk of the refrigerator room. From their vantage point across the warehouse, they had an unrestricted view of the delivery bay rolling door that scrolled up and allowed trucks to back right up to the warehouse floor to unload the cargo.

The room was bathed in darkness. The only illumination was spotlights fixed on the rolling door and the doorways that led to the unrefrigerated section of the warehouse where the boxed food was stored.

The catwalk was a tight fit, so Keisha was seated

between Shane's legs, his thighs bracketing hers and her butt up against his crotch.

Shane had been a close observer to the inner workings of Keisha's brilliant and convoluted mind. She hid her soft center, encased that marshmallow heart in a hard attitude that fooled most of the world.

He wasn't going to lie. At one point, he'd been a little bit scared of her. She was a Ball Buster with a capital BB. But ever since Keisha had revealed that inner softness, Shane had been dying to see that gooey, sweet woman again.

The last time she'd shown him had been when they rescued Maria Torres. She'd focused right in on Maria's pain and her fear and done everything to put her at ease and mother her.

And while he had no interest in Keisha mothering him, none at all, he wanted, with a fierce passion, to see that soft woman again.

He'd almost blown it this morning. Of course, he had no idea what he'd done wrong. All he'd done was get out of bed, unashamed of the erection she inspired. He'd mentioned his Go Bag, but why that would have garnered hostility was beyond him.

She'd been pissed. And as far as he could tell, he hadn't necessarily done anything to change her mind. But she had, and then offered to join him.

He should have been completely wrung out after three rounds of very energetic and long lasting sex. But from the moment he'd awoken with her ass pressed against him, all he could think about was getting inside her again.

They'd managed another round in the shower, and when they'd left her apartment, they'd both been sated and happy.

If only he could keep her chained up and in bed. Life would be perfect.

And wow, would he get his balls handed to him if he even voiced that thought out loud. He chuckled softly.

"What are you laughing at?"

"Would you bust my balls if I said I was imagining you chained to my bed?"

Keisha should probably be offended at the image, but after working with Shane over the past few months, she knew that he respected her in the field. He might be a pain in the ass sometimes, but he'd ultimately supported her decisions when they'd protected Maria Torres. And he'd followed her lead several times today.

As a matter of fact, they'd worked the day seamlessly, instinctively knowing when one was actually snooping, the other would keep the volunteers at the food bank occupied.

And while they'd worked well together, in bed they were even more compatible. Shane seemed to have an instinctive ability to know exactly how far he could push. And Keisha trusted him to take her to the edge, shoving her past former comfort zones, yet she knew he would never hurt her.

As a result, Keisha had never been so satiated. Shane's chest was thick and solid behind her. And she felt as if she could just lay down in a puddle of satisfaction and never get up again. She fought the urge to rub against him like a cat in heat.

She couldn't keep her hands off him. And apparently since he wanted to chain her to the bed, the feeling was mutual.

"Lucky for you I'm unbelievably relaxed right now." But her tone promised future retribution.

Shane chuckled. "Can't wait."

The chill temperatures did little to cool the fire that

raged in her blood. He'd turned her into a raving sex maniac. All she could think about was getting this surveillance out of the way and heading back to her condo so they could go at it again.

She was trying to keep her head because she knew this would end. Likely soon. She would still have to work with him so it couldn't end badly.

"You warm enough?" He had wrapped her in his arms and rubbed at her forearms.

"Yeah." Keisha held the Nikon D4 with the AF-S NIKKOR 14-24mm wide angle zoom lens. If Bob Michaels was correct, there would be another clandestine shipment tonight.

The information had come in late this afternoon. The broccoli had tested positive for a banned pesticide. So whoever was donating the food didn't want the tainted food to be linked to their farm.

The strange thing about this whole situation was that the food bank didn't really have any protocol in place for produce donations. They had just been worried because whoever was delivering the food was doing it under cover of the night which seemed to indicate some sort of foul play. Which turned out to be the case.

In the meantime, the food bank had to protect the recipients of their food. Which meant all that broccoli needed to be destroyed and the culprits needed to be caught and stopped.

The food bank was in a delicate position. They couldn't openly ask who was giving them late night deliveries. If they publicly acknowledged that they didn't know where it came from, it could incite the customers to stop requesting food until they verified the food was safe. Going hungry was better than eating tainted produce.

Keisha settled in the crook of Shane's arms and watched the puff of white as she breathed.

"So a thong woman, huh?"

Keisha blushed but damned if she'd truly be embarrassed. "Ever since I got out of the Navy. You know what they make us wear?"

Shane chuckled. "I may have had eyes on those grannie skivvies once or twice."

Probably more than once or twice. Keisha tried not to let the thought bother her. "Yeah, well they are hideous. So now I indulge my inner vixen with my Victoria's Secret credit card."

"And your inner vixen is my favorite." Shane's arms tightened around her. "What'cha wearing right now?"

She softened as his voice coiled low and seductive through her body. "Wouldn't you like to know." She'd put on a particularly sexy demi-bra and matching thong in a pearly pastel pink.

"I'm planning to find out when we're done here." Shane slid his palms underneath the hem of her jacket and up the front of her shirt until he found her nipples hard and aching for his touch. He plucked at the nubs and Keisha smiled in satisfaction as his erection prodded her back.

"I put on my skimpiest thong just for you," she purred.

"Damn, girl." He spread his legs a little wider and pinched her nipples. Just hard enough to sting but without an edge of pain.

For such a large man he had a very delicate and precise touch.

They knew they couldn't exactly have sex on the catwalk, but they could fool around a little. Shane continued to play with her nipples and Keisha reached behind her and

pressed her palm over the thick bulge of his cock in his cargo pants.

She went a little light-headed at how big and hard he was, still not used to his girth or length. Her last few lovers had been significantly smaller than Shane.

Her heart beat against her breastbone as they teased each other. The only sound in the silent warehouse was their deepening breaths as they kept each other on the edge.

Shane nuzzled her ear. "Hold that thought." The metal door to the delivery bay began to roll up. Both Shane and Keisha sat up straight, their focus on the intruder, sex pushed to the side but not forgotten. "Later, I'm going to do everything I want to you and you're going to take it."

Keisha's breath caught, held. Until later. And she'd do the same to him. Screw it. She'd worry about future heartache…in the future. "Right back at you."

The soft rumble of a truck backing up to the door infiltrated the darkness of the refrigerated room.

As soon as the truck breached the threshold, the driver stopped and the distinctive sound of the gear being set in park hit their ears.

Someone hopped out of the passenger side of the cab and headed directly for the light switch that would illuminate the entire refrigerated compartment. Keisha held the camera up, tracked their movements through the lens viewer, and waited for the moment when they'd finally see who was clandestinely filling Food for Life's pantry with tainted food.

As the light switched on and a very familiar red-head came into view, Keisha swore softly.

"Who is it?" Shane leaned around to get a better look at the intruder. "Shit, is that—"

Shelley.

Jack's mother. Stepmother. Whatever. The woman who practically raised him and who Jack had nothing but admiration for was delivering tainted produce to the Food for Life warehouse.

Keisha continued to snap incriminating photos of Shelley as she directed the driver of the truck who was still covered in a light film of dirt. There were several spaces open, and using the forklift, they were able to seamlessly move the bulk bins filled with broccoli, clearly harvested straight from the fields, from the truck into those open slots.

Shelley propped her hands on her hips and frowned at the previously delivered pallets of broccoli. She clearly recognized that the bins they'd delivered the other day hadn't been boxed and distributed.

A sick sensation settled in the pit of Keisha's stomach. How the hell were they going to tell Jack that his mother was involved?

Keisha hid behind the technical aspects of shooting the misconduct taking place, ignoring the reality that something was very, very wrong. And ignoring the fact that she and Shane were going to have to deliver some very bad news to her boss.

CHAPTER 6

They sat in Shane's Charger, neither saying a word as they contemplated the complete cluster fuck that tonight had turned into. Keisha dreaded this phone call but it had to be done.

She pressed 2 on her speed dial and waited for Jack to pick up.

"You got them."

"Jack—"

"Did you call Bob Michaels?"

"I, we, thought you'd want to see the evidence first."

"Keisha, what the hell is going on?" Jack's voice had gotten quieter. A sure sign that he was beginning to comprehend that something was seriously wrong.

"It's complicated." Keisha glanced at Shane, his large bulk dominated the driver's seat of the sports car. "Can I come over?"

"We," Shane said.

"You want to come over now?" The covers rustled and Jack murmured, "Go back to sleep, love." Then there was a click of a door closing.

"I think that would be best."

"Okay." Jack said, "Use the gate code, it's the reverse of the office security code."

"See you in half an hour." Keisha pushed the off button on her cell. "You don't have to go with me."

Although she didn't have her car. Shane had insisted they take his because he wouldn't fit comfortably in her ten year old Honda Civic. Even though her car definitely would not stand out in this industrial area. Not like Shane's did.

"Of course I do."

"Then let's get to it."

Shane shifted the rumbling engine into drive and they took off.

Keisha's heart beat with a sick rhythm. Because she couldn't come up with any possible good reason why Jack's mother, stepmother, whatever, would be delivering tainted produce to the local food bank in the middle of the night.

The trek to the house on Seventeen Mile Drive had been accomplished in a charged silence. Shane parked in the circular drive across from the wide stone steps that lead to the elegant porch. Once Shane shut the engine off, the only noise in the early morning hour was the shush of the ocean waves hitting the rocks in their cove. Even the seagulls and seals were silent.

Shane had known the route to Jack's family home. "You've been here before?"

"For certain clients, my service occasionally extends to pickups or drop offs at their house."

Keisha nodded.

"How about you?"

"Company holiday party." Keisha's stomach roiled again as she thought about how nice and welcoming Shelley had been. Keisha had been a little awestruck by the size and opulence of the Stone Mansion. In actuality the furnishings weren't super fancy but the house was a sprawling monstrosity with an ornate two story entrance, seven bedrooms, and the entire back of the house was walls of windows with incredible views of the Pacific. But Shelley had put her at ease, sharing her own reaction the first time she viewed the ocean from the house.

Keisha curled her fingers around the chrome door handle. "Let's get this over with."

Shane nodded and they exited the car.

Jack had the massive front doors open before they even breached the porch. "Jesus, you two look like you're going to a funeral. It can't be that bad." He had tugged on a ragged pair of grey sweat pants and a wrinkled white t-shirt, and wore a small grin.

Keisha and Shane strode into the grand entryway. A massive chandelier hung over a fancy Persian rug that probably cost more than her car…when it was new.

Keisha clutched the expensive, highly accurate digital camera, her fingers tight with the effort to hold in her worry.

"Let's go into the kitchen." Jack lead them into the casual, welcoming warmth of the center of the house. He gestured to the long mahogany plank table and they sat in silence with Jack at the head and Shane and Keisha flanking him on either side. "Let's have it."

Keisha pulled up the shots of Shelley in the warehouse and handed the camera silently to her boss and friend.

He'd long since lost his smile, but he wasn't pissed…he was frowning. He went through the set of fifty time-stamped digital pictures, once then twice. One hand rubbed the center of his chest while he analyzed the evidence.

"I'm sorry Jack." Shane's voice rumbled from his chest.

"There's got to be something else going on here." Jack

shook his head. His hair stood straight up but his sleepy eyes were now sharp as he flipped through the pictures again. "I know this looks bad."

"Didn't you say the results came back on the produce?" Keisha asked and resisted the urge to wrap her arm around his wide shoulders. She knew how awful it was when someone you trusted let you down.

"Yeah." Jack rubbed his palm over his hair until it stood up. "But Shelley wouldn't do something like this."

"Sometimes, people let you down," Keisha said softly.

Shane watched the quiet drama between Keisha and Jack, keeping his mouth shut.

He didn't know Jack's stepmother well but he would certainly keep an open mind until all the facts were in. Of course the evidence looked damning, but hell, this was Jack Stone's mother. Not his biological mother, but the woman who came to live here when Jack was fourteen. She became the sole parent of three basically orphaned boys and her daughter, because sure as shit, Jack's father hadn't given a rat's ass about his kids.

But this moment had given him the opportunity to see Keisha's soft side again. She had exposed that gooey, marshmallow center and was patting Jack's hand, her voice firm yet compassionate as she tried to comfort him. As she spoke, Shane had to wonder who had let her down so badly she didn't even entertain the thought that Shelley was innocent, because clearly she spoke from experience.

"You've got to accept that Shelley let you down and start dealing with it."

"I hear what you're saying Keish, but you don't know my mom." Jack drummed his fingers over his lips and stared at a gleaming polished mahogany bowl filled with red and pink foil-wrapped candy hearts.

Keisha blinked and sent an imploring look Shane's way, as if saying 'talk some sense into the crazy man'.

"You've got to let the food bank know we found the culprit," Keisha said more firmly.

"We need to talk to her first." Jack nodded. "Get her side of the story before we convict her."

Before Shane could interject, the entry door from the garage into the kitchen swung open.

Shelley tiptoed inside. She seemed to note the kitchen lights were on at the same time she realized that Jack, Keisha, and Shane sat at the kitchen table. And Shane sure couldn't help but think that for a moment she looked guilty as hell.

Shelley stopped abruptly her red hair swung around her shoulders. She closed her eyelids over her striking green eyes. She had been young when she'd had Jess so she was only about ten years older than Jack. She clearly took care of herself. She could easily pass for a woman in her thirties.

She had a look of utter surprise on her face, which then morphed into a sheepish grin. "Busted."

"Hi Shel," Jack said softly.

"Well, this is certainly an odd time to be entertaining." Shelley bustled into the kitchen and headed for the refrigerator. "Jack, you didn't even offer your guests something to drink."

"It isn't a social call, Shel."

"Oh. Oh," she drew out the word as her green eyes widened. "Sorry to interrupt then. I'll just go on up to bed."

"Actually this concerns you." Jack sounded grim.

"Me?" her voice squeaked.

"Have a seat." Jack pushed one of the heavy wood chairs out from the table, the scrape and screech against the Saltillo tiles loud in the very silent room. "We need to talk."

"Well, doesn't this sound serious." Shelley tried to joke but Shane noted exactly when she realized that no one else was smiling.

Shane kept a close eye on Keisha, trying to figure out who could have hurt her so badly that she'd automatically assume that Shelley was guilty. Of course, the current evidence would suggest that to be true. But it wasn't logical.

He and Jack had had enough conversations about their mothers that Shane knew that Jack wouldn't believe that Shelley was guilty until he had incontrovertible proof or her confession.

After she sat in the chair, Jack handed the camera to his mom.

Keisha now stood by the back French doors, arms crossed over her chest. Her body language was so defensive that it was a wonder that she didn't bust out a weapon and try to remand Shelley into custody.

"Oh dear." Shelley leaned back in the chair, her posture relaxed as if she'd snuck a cookie before dinner, not delivered tainted produce to be distributed to the unsuspecting working poor. "You caught me."

Keisha was nodding, her lush lips pressed in to a flat, disapproving line.

Shane wondered if he should make Jack leave the room. Because they couldn't afford to go easy on Shelley if they wanted to get to the bottom of this. "Maybe you should take a break, Jack," Shane said ominously.

Jack shook his head. "I'm good."

Shane took a deep breath and settled into a zone. She was no longer Shelley, Jack's mother, she was an enemy combatant whose actions could jeopardize lives. With each inhale, he increased his bulk, tensing his muscles, expanding until his body was an unmistakable physical threat.

"What exactly did we catch you doing?" Shane's tone brooked no excuses. He hardened his heart and his voice.

Shelley handed the camera back to Jack and pressed her hand over her stepson's. "It's a little silly." She still wasn't showing an appropriate level of fear for the situation. Shane had caused grown men to break with just his bulk and yet Shelley was still treating the situation as a minor infraction rather than the serious crime that it was. Something definitely wasn't right.

Keisha huffed out a disgusted breath.

"Mom," Jack said gently.

Too nice. She needed to be worried not cajoled. Shane silently indicated to Jack to shut up. "Start at the beginning."

"I started a farm co-op with some money I got recently from your father."

So far she hadn't said anything that would be admissible and she still wasn't getting the seriousness of her actions.

Shane knew he needed to do something to up the intimidation factor. He carefully pried her fingers from Jack's hand and pressed her palm flat against the table.

"And…?" Shane hated to make her uncomfortable. But he narrowed his gaze and waited.

Shelley licked her lips and it finally seemed as if she was starting to comprehend that she was in trouble. Her gaze darted between Shane and Jack, who hadn't said a word when Shane had disengaged their hands.

"We bought the land a few months ago. Prepped, planted. We've got several full time employees and just harvested our first crop of broccoli a few weeks ago." Her smile was tentative as if waiting for approval. "And we've delivered thousands of pounds of nutritious vegetables to Food for Life."

So far, Shelley hadn't said a word about the fact that they'd used illegal pesticides. Shane was getting a very bad feeling about this. He shot Jack a questioning look. His eyebrows raised. Did Jack want him to continue?

Jack dipped his chin, and watched his stepmother.

"I don't understand why you are so upset."

Shane shot back. "Why deliver under cover of the night?"

"Well, we wanted the donations to be anonymous, rather than making a big deal of the fact that we were contributing more."

Keisha snorted.

And Shelley crossed her arms across her waist, seeming to hug herself.

"You realize that your actions could be construed as trying to hide evidence of your wrongdoing."

"Evidence?" Shelley's voice rose and she straightened up, her tone getting defensive. Finally. "You're making it sound like I'm a criminal."

"So you had no idea that the produce you delivered has been sprayed with banned substances."

"What banned chemicals?" But Shelley didn't let them answer. "No! That can't be possible."

Keisha spoke, "Aldicarb."

Shelley was shaking her head. "That's illegal. It can't be used on broccoli."

"You had no idea?" Keisha's derisive comeback shot out of her mouth and Shane could see the moment when she realized she had just basically accused her boss's mother of illegal activity.

"Of course not," Shelley said indignantly, liquid shimmered in her eyes.

"Mom this is important." Jack squeezed her fingers. "You had no knowledge of illegal activity?"

"I would never jeopardize the health of the recipients of our food." Shelley stood abruptly, shoving back her chair so violently that it tipped over and would have fallen if Keisha hadn't grabbed the back. "The goal was to get more healthy food onto the plates of people who need it."

"Okay. Okay." Jack tried to placate her.

"You're sure you didn't know?" Keisha said one more time but her eyes had softened and she was about ready to wrap Shelley in a comforting hug. Shane was fascinated to see that caretaker, that soft-centered woman, come barreling out of the tough cookie that she'd been only minutes ago.

"Who authorized the spray?" Jack asked urgently.

"I have no idea."

They still weren't any closer to finding the culprit. "Who's your co-op partner?"

"Don Wallaston."

The smarmy guy who had leered at Keisha's hickey? Shane didn't like the guy but that didn't mean he was a criminal. "Would he have access to the illegal pesticide?"

"I don't know. That substance was banned by the FDA on certain types of fruits and vegetables years ago." Shelley seemed hesitant. "But he does own a corporate farm. He supplies several types of produce to Del Monte."

"So he could potentially have had access to it?"

"I guess. It would have to have been purchased a while ago," Shelley replied drily. "But yes, it is possible. He'd have more access than I would."

"He couldn't use the pesticide on his own farm's crops." Jack said, "All the registered commercial crops are tested regularly for illegal pesticides. The incidence of illegal chemicals has been all but eradicated here."

"But it doesn't make any sense." Shelley pursed her lips. "I do the finances for our little co-op and we bought and used the correct approved pest repellents. We actually argued about this because I wanted to go organic but Don insisted that our crop yield would be better with the chemicals. So I gave in."

Jack asked, "If he switched the banned substance with the allowed substance he would have a use or outlet for the allowable pesticides you purchased."

"I'm not sure I follow," Shelley said reluctantly.

"Say he had some Aldicarb gathering dust at his corporate farm and he knew he couldn't use it. This was the perfect way to get rid of the chemicals. He'd save on the purchase of legal pesticides and then substitute the illegal for the legal and use the correct safe pesticide at his corporate farm."

"That's awful." Shelley reluctantly admitted, "But possible."

"We need to find out where those chemicals came from and who authorized the use of the pesticide."

"Oh, my God." Shelley put her hand to her forehead. "We've got to get that produce out of the warehouse before it's distributed to the public."

Jack stood and wrapped his arms around his mother. "Don't worry. Luckily Bob Michaels wanted to test the produce before he started delivering it."

"Wait, so you investigated the food bank?" she asked as if she were just putting all the pieces together.

Jack shrugged. "Actually, Shane and Keisha were undercover at the wine and dine the other night."

"I thought I saw you!" Shelley's eyes watered and she blinked rapidly. "Do you really think that Don Wallaston would have authorized the use of an illegal substance on produce for the hungry?"

Shit, Shane did not want to deal with tears.

"It's either him or you." Keisha snarked.

"Now, Shelley. We are going to nail that sucker." Shane had gentled his voice, and softened his tone, wanting her to settle. He'd been pretty sure she hadn't had direct knowledge of the tainted produce and now that they knew for sure, Shane's job was to protect her. Keisha was staring at him with an enigmatic look on her face.

"How?"

That was a good question. Because they needed to proceed carefully. They had to make sure that they caught the culprit either without implicating Jack's mother or with a way to clear her, because right now Shelley was still considered culpable.

Keisha patted Shelley on the back, trying to comfort her, as if to make up for the fact that she had earlier believed that Shelley was guilty. "Don't you worry, Shelley. Jack, Shane, and I are going to get him."

Jack said, "Go on to bed. I'll let you know if we need your help with anything."

Shelley wiped the wetness from beneath her eyes and nodded. After she left the room, Jack sighed heavily. "Unless we can get Wallaston to confess, she's fucked."

"So let's get him to confess." But Shane knew they were going to have to come up with a plan and no matter how he twisted things around, they were likely going to have to use Shelley as bait.

CHAPTER 7

"Well, that was fun." Shane rubbed his large palm over his bald head and huffed out a breath as they walked to his car. "Let me get you home."

And maybe while he had her captive in his car, he could delve into the workings of her mind. Then once he'd discovered her secrets, he'd move on to exploring her body and they'd engage in a repeat of their incredible sexual chemistry from last night.

He mentally snorted.

Shane started the car, headed out of Seventeen Mile Drive and toward the highway. The car was filled with an easy silence as they both contemplated their thoughts.

"You were good with her," Keisha said. "I mean it."

"I felt like a big bully."

"We needed to know for sure if she was involved."

He'd been rough on Shelley at first but it had been necessary. And while he'd managed to get the information by being scary, he'd eased off once they had her 'confession'.

"You thought she was guilty." Shane kept the statement as noncommittal as possible, trying hard not to piss Keisha

58

off. But he really wanted to understand her. Wanted to know what made her react the way she did in every situation.

"Yes."

"Why did you assume she was guilty?" He glanced at her as he took the bend in Highway 1, juicing the engine and increasing his speed.

"People let you down." Keisha shrugged. "I try to believe the worst, and be surprised by the best."

Shane shifted his attention back to the road. People let you down. People. Before tonight, he would have thought she meant men, but now he perceived it was more than just a disappointment in men. "Parents?"

"Maybe."

"My mama *never* let me down." Shane emphasized never. Because it was true.

"And what about your father?"

"Never knew him."

"Left before you were born?" Keisha asked. "Like mine."

He'd take that out and examine it later. She expected his father to be a deserter. "No. He was killed in a drive-by shooting. The bullet was meant for a gang banger walking past his house. Unfortunately, it ricocheted, went through the living room window, and pierced his heart." Shane rubbed his hand over his chest to ease the ache that never seemed to go away.

The physical ache was a sadness for his mother. For Shane, it was hard to miss someone he'd never known, but his mother had never gotten over his father's death.

"Oh." Keisha laid her palm over his wrist, her fingers delicate compared to his larger thicker bones. The simple contact zapped straight to his groin. His cock swelled with desire as she turned that sweetness on him. "I'm so sorry for your mother."

"Yeah. She never got over him."

"So, she never got together with anyone else?"

"She's had a few men friends." Shane winced. He really didn't like to think of his mother that way, which was head-in-the-sand silly of him. She was a grown woman. But she was still his mama.

"So why are you such a player?"

He'd grown up with a mother who pined for her dead lover for years. He had no intention of giving away his heart and winding up sad and alone and filled with heartache. The truth was, forever came with a lot of pain.

So many people had clearly let Keisha down, and he ought to be honest, but this was a subject he'd avoided for years. So he did what he always did and tossed off another truth that was far less revealing. "Because no one could ever compare to my mama."

Shane shut down the engine. They were in the parking lot of Keisha's condo building. It was late. She was illuminated in the shimmering moonlight with her tough clothes, black combat boots, black cargo pants, and a tight black athletic wear shirt that emphasized her round, high breasts and the flat plane of her stomach. She looked like a bad ass.

But underneath the slick material he could see the satin and lace of her bra.

And he remembered that earlier, before everything that happened with Shelley, he'd had his hands on those breasts and she'd promised him a viewing of her underwear.

Shane leaned toward the passenger seat and nuzzled the long column of her neck. He pressed wet openmouthed kisses along her shoulder and eased the tight material aside to catch a glimpse of a pale pink bra strap. The sweet pearly pink was at odds with her tough clothes and her bad ass vibe.

"You gonna invite me in and show me more of your Victoria's Secret obsession?" He smiled against her shoulder and prayed she wouldn't kick him to the curb. A sultry musk and the scent of patchouli and lemon rose from her skin.

Memories from last night cascaded in his mind and his body reacted as if they were both naked and tangled in her sheets. Right where he wanted to be again tonight. He wanted to have sex with her all night long. Again.

He was pretty sure that was all he'd get from her.

He thought about how she'd comforted Shelley. After Keisha was convinced of Shelley's innocence she'd once again revealed that soft center. And Shane finally realized that the only way to get her to open that gooey center was to be vulnerable. That wasn't ever going to happen, because his sense of self-preservation was far greater than his wish to have her turn that sweetness on him. But he'd take another night of sex if she'd give it to him.

Keisha was silent but she wasn't pushing him away. And her non-reaction gave him hope. If he wasn't mistaken she'd just tilted her head a little to the right to give him better access to the sweet spot behind her ear.

Shane pressed a kiss against her skin, gratified by the sensual shiver that shook her body. Uneasy with his urgent need, he fought his near desperation for her, even as he considered how to get her to agree to let him spend the night.

Keisha shivered. Her nipples sharpened into hard bullets pressing against the delicate lace and tight Under Armour with almost painful intensity. God, she wanted to invite him in.

Repeat last night. Over and over.

The sex had been amazing, energetic, and physical. He would wear her out and she'd be unable to worry about the consequences of having him spend a second night in a row at her place.

Keisha still had her fists clenched against her thighs, fighting the urge to clutch his head to her breast. Somehow she knew that if she touched him, she would be lost. The only place they had contact was Shane's fingers curled on her top's neckline and his mouth against her collarbone.

She wanted to give in. Wanted to lose herself in sex, in him. Even though she knew it was a bad idea because it wasn't just about sex anymore. They had connected on another level beyond the physical. And she wasn't sure her heart could stand the pain when they were over. But her heart overruled her head and even though she knew it was a terrible idea, she gave in. "Let's go inside."

"Hot damn," he breathed against her neck. Shane pressed the unlock button on her seatbelt, freeing her from the safety restraint.

The dark thrill in his voice was gratifying. She didn't want to regret tonight. They still had to run the sting tomorrow. But their undercover operation as husband and wife was already mostly over. She could rationalize that the more comfortable they were together the easier the sell to get Don Wallaston to confess would be. But the truth was it didn't matter if he bought their fake marriage.

Shane reached for the glove box. "Okay if I bring my weapon inside?"

Keisha glanced down at the bulge in his cargo pants. "I don't think you can leave it here."

Shane snorted. "Funny. I meant my gun."

"Of course." Keisha was still chuckling over her joke

when he took her mouth like a conquering invader. He ate at her lips like a starving man at a banquet. Keisha's heart quickened and her lady parts combusted. One hand cupped her breast firmly through the sleek material of her shirt. He brushed his thumb back and forth over her distended nipple until she moaned into his mouth.

Keisha shoved the tight material of his shirt up so that that she could run her hands along his hot, smooth skin, his abs rippled at her light contact. Desire rose between them like searing summer heat on a shimmering blacktop.

The gearshift dug into her side as Shane half lifted her up so that he could scrape his teeth over her neck and down the sensitive curve of her breast before suckling her tight nipple into his mouth right through the clingy material.

Keisha undid the snap on his pants and got his zipper down in record time. Shane grunted as she reached inside and found his bare cock. Commando, good lord.

Damn. She'd forgotten how big he was as she wrapped her hand around his thick length and pumped twice. A drop of pre-come was hot on her palm.

Shane stopped, rested his forehead against her collarbone. "It's fucking amazing how hot you get me in such a short amount of time."

"Give me a few more minutes and you'll be even hotter," she promised.

He huffed out a laugh. "The front seat of my car was not made for a man my size to get it on."

"Come on," Keisha said with a strange desperation. Her body was aching, on fire, empty and she needed him inside her. "Be adventurous."

"Babe." Shane groaned. "We've got to get inside."

"You. Inside me. Now." She rolled through the gap between the front and back seats and shimmied her pants down to her ankles, but her combat boots stopped her progress.

"I really want to take my time and enjoy that underwear." Shane was trying to hold out against her desperate need but when she splayed her legs on the leather backseat, her top wet from his mouth, and her scent rising from the pale pink triangle of lace that covered her mound, she knew she had him. As his gaze dropped to her pussy, she watched him lose the battle.

"Enjoy it later."

Shane climbed through the opening, fairly smoothly for a man his size. His cock jutted from the open V of his pants, thick, wide, pre-come beading on the dark tip.

And she moaned.

Her whole body clenched at the sight of his magnificent muscled abs and the knowledge that very soon he would be buried deep inside her weeping sex.

"Babe." He rolled a condom on. "I can't believe we're going to do this twenty feet from your front door."

"Now."

Shane pushed aside the pearly pink thong, his fingers coated with her slickness, and Keisha moaned again. Then he slid home.

There was no other word for it.

Her pants hobbled her legs and made it difficult to spread wide. As he rocked in and out of her slick heat, his cock hit all of her zones, her g-spot, her clit. His hips rocked hard against her partially open thighs, effectively bracketing him.

He knelt between her legs, his feet hung over the edge of the seat, and his shoulders blocked out all the light from the parking lot, bathing his face in shadows.

His expression was fierce as he braced one arm on the

back head rest and slid his large palm under her ass. Then he lifted her, changing the angle of penetration and suddenly Keisha hurtled over the edge as she flew apart and disintegrated into a million little pieces. She contracted around his thick invasive cock, and Shane groaned and stiffened. She rejoiced as he flew with her. His cock pulsed inside her, his head thrown back, his muscles tight, gripped in the throes of release.

Her heart was pounding so loudly it was a wonder she didn't wake the neighbors.

Shane was breathing hard as if he'd just run the O course in record time.

"Damn, babe." He brushed a stray lock of hair from her sweat dampened cheek and then nuzzled her neck in an uncharacteristic display of sweetness. "You about killed me."

The windows were fogged and the interior of the car was scented with them. The sweet musk of Shane, Keisha, and explosive sex.

She inhaled deeply and held the scent inside her trying to commit this moment to her memory banks. Little tremors still rocked her, his semi-hard cock inside her, his rough hairy thighs between her softer ones, his balls snugged tight against her swollen sex, the restriction of her pants around her ankles, and the contraction of his stomach muscles against hers as he basically held an extended pushup.

His bunched biceps were as thick as her thighs, and his chest was wider than her door frame. The brother was built. She was no giant, but his bulk made her feel almost delicate, feminine.

Shane groaned again. And although she'd like to think it was her sexy personality. She was pretty sure he needed to move from his contorted position. "You need to move?"

"Hell, no. Let's stay like this all night." He nuzzled her again. "If I could keep you locked up back here, naked and sweet and open, I'd do it in a heartbeat."

The words should have pushed her buttons, gotten her back up. But his rough admission just made her want to start on round two. "Why don't we continue this conversation inside?" Her voice had softened as she thought about how uncomfortable he must be right now.

Her butt was stuck to the leather seat and her back was about to start cramping.

"I thought you'd never ask." Shane smiled and Keisha's heart tumbled. "God I love that sweetness. I love that you just turned it on me."

It was too late to try to bring back the attitude. She'd have it back in place tomorrow but right now, his sweet was working for her too.

With a silent, unexpected thud, she fell. She knew better and still she wanted to believe him. Wanted to trust that softness, that gentleness in his words, and wish that he'd be there for her forever, that she could count on him not to let her down.

CHAPTER 8

The next morning, Keisha strode to Shane's Charger, putting a little extra swing in her hips since she knew he was behind her. Her high heels clicked against the asphalt in a confident rhythm. Last night had been amazing. Again.

He groaned. "You're trying to kill me."

She let her lips curl and a lightness filled her. She felt good. Happy. She tossed a saucy look over her shoulder and felt like laughing. Her. Laughing.

"If the shoe fits...."

"Those shoes should be illegal." Shane had sidled up behind her, his body molded behind hers, one thick forearm wrapped around her waist, his chest warm against her back and her butt snugged up against his groin. "Later, I want to see you in just that pale yellow lace bra and panty set and those pumps. Then I'm going to fuck you against the wall."

Her whole body softened and her sex went wet at his words. That was the reason they were late this morning.

They'd gotten distracted when he'd come out of the bathroom with only a towel wrapped around his waist, water droplets sprinkled on his skin. And she'd been half dressed in her pastel yellow lace demi bra that pushed her breasts up and together accenting her cleavage, a matching thong, and her snakeskin pumps with a pale yellow heel that matched her lingerie. She knew they made her legs look good.

They'd taken one look at each other and within seconds, he'd had her flat on the bed, and was buried inside her while her heels dug into his butt and he powered in and out of her.

Keisha's knees went weak at the memory. "Sounds good," she said breathlessly.

They slid into the car. Shane looked pretty good himself. He'd replenished his Go Bag sometime yesterday, and was wearing khakis, a white button down that emphasized the burnished ebony of his skin, and penny loafers.

"Pop the glove box and put this inside for me, would you babe?" He handed her his weapon and then started the car.

She opened the glove box and that's when she saw it. When the sexual glow from last night, and this morning, evaporated in a searing moment of pain. The diamond earring sparkled in the warm light from inside the glove box. The woman's jewelry was a glaring visual reminder that Shane Washington was a player.

She pressed her lips together and her mouth turned down.

"What's wrong?" Shane had instantly intuited her change in mood. He clasped her chin gently and turned her head so that she was forced to look at him.

"Nothing." Her body was stiff as she continued to process the implications of that earring. "We're already late. We should get going."

"Babe. I know you. It's not nothing."

Keisha blinked slowly, tried to hide her emotions from

him. He didn't know her. He knew the her that gave in to his charm and her own traitorous body. Not the her that protected her heart at all costs. "Maybe I'm just prepping for this takedown." It was going to be a delicate situation.

"That's not it either."

"Fine. I was just reminded that you're a player."

"Why are you bringing that up again? Because our sex is off that charts?" he asked with frustration. "It's off the charts because of us, together. We combust."

"I'm sure you…combust with plenty of women."

"Jesus, Keish. I'm with you right now." But then as if he realized that she'd backed off when she opened the glove box, Shane peered inside. "What did you see?"

Keisha shrugged.

But Shane wouldn't let it go. She should have known he'd be a bull dog when it came to getting to the bottom of her attempted dismissal.

He didn't even seem to see the incriminating evidence. "Come on, Keish. At least give me the courtesy of an answer, and a chance to defend myself against whatever perceived problem you've got with me now."

"Why do you care?" she snapped.

"Hell if I know. But I do," Shane snapped right back. "Tell. Me."

Finally she recognized the determination in his narrowed gaze, relented, and just told him what was bothering her. "The earring."

"What about it?"

"You can't be that obtuse," she said.

"It belongs to a client," Shane said with exasperation. "She's one of the clients who gets extra service. I do a lot of business with her company. I dropped her *and her husband* off at home after they got back from a business trip to San

Francisco. Then I found it in the backseat when I was cleaning my car."

Keisha stayed quiet. She'd jumped to conclusions. But maybe that was just her brain trying to spare her future heartache. Because she was pretty sure that she was in too deep to totally avoid pain.

"Hey," Shane said gruffly. "Next time. Ask me. Don't just assume."

Next time. As if there would be a next time. Keisha crossed her arms over her chest, she knew the posture was defensive but she was feeling the need to protect herself any way she could.

"There will be a next time," Shane insisted. "Okay?"

"We'd better get on the road."

He sighed and put the car in gear.

And she knew this discussion wasn't over.

THEY ENTERED the offices of Food for Life only a few minutes late.

The offices were built in a small corner of the warehouse. The walls had been painted a cheery pale teal, and gray linoleum covered the cold industrial cement floor. In the middle of the room, two standard office desks with fake wood veneer circa 1970 faced each other, and the wall was lined with old metal filing cabinets. A bulletin board, pinned with flyers printed on neon paper advertising the various fundraisers and donation days, was on the wall right inside the door.

On the same wall as the door were two large windows with a view of the parking lot and the semi-trucks ready to be loaded with shrink-wrapped pallets of boxed food. Shane put a proprietary hand in the small of Keisha's back, determined to let everyone know she was his. Silly, but the move was the civilized man's equivalent of the caveman marking his territory.

"Good afternoon, Mr. and Mrs. Washington." Monica Peterson was dressed to work in the warehouse but the rest of the room's occupants were in business suits. And while Shane could care less about fitting in and the 'uniform' of the casually wealthy, he knew that this group would take him more seriously if he looked like one of them.

Keisha had obviously thought the same. Dressed in her black suit, short black skirt, tight pale yellow cami, a crop black jacket and those killer pumps she projected class and confidence. He loved her in her black cargo pants and tight Under Armour, but those pumps seriously kicked up his heart rate. He vowed he was going to have those shoes digging into his butt another time.

Shelley was there looking fairly nervous. Shane tried to give her a reassuring smile but he wasn't positive it worked when she blanched and ran a hand down her tan skirt.

Bob Michaels, the Chairman, kept clicking his pen. He'd been informed that they'd identified the culprit but they didn't tell him who it was. They needed the edge of surprise so they could get Wallaston to confess.

Jack Stone had come as backup but his main priority was to protect Shelley.

"Why don't we all get more comfortable," Bob Michaels suggested. They'd prepped him ahead of time so that he'd know they wanted everyone corralled into one room. "Let's head into the conference room."

One by one they shuffled into the long rectangular room. Unlike the outer office, the floor in the conference room was carpeted, likely to muffle the sound. Jack had already set up electronic measures to capture the confession on audio and had a highly sensitive microphone taped to his chest. Precautionary tactics in case this got ugly.

Shane couldn't imagine that anyone in this room was all that dangerous but with Keisha next to him, he wasn't about to take any chances.

Keisha and Shane sat, and turned down offers of coffee, soda, or water.

"Now, Mr. Washington, you mentioned some concerns on the phone," Mrs. Peterson led the discussion.

"Yes." Shane confirmed. "First off, I wanted to say thank you for being so accommodating as to meet with us today. My travel schedule is unpredictable, and Keisha and I like to make decisions together." He shot an adoring glance at her.

Instead of her trademark sass, she only narrowed her eyes and smiled before turning to the other members in the room. "We were very impressed with your operation, the scope of the clients that you serve, even the efficiency of your volunteers," Keisha said precisely and sweetly. But Shane knew that soft voice was the precursor to words so sharp they could cut.

However her words were all true. After their time working here yesterday, Shane was planning on making that donation to the food bank.

"And what did you think?" Don Wallaston directed his comment to Shane, completely dismissing Keisha.

Shelley paled and Shane knew this was where they needed to be very careful.

"We were disturbed to find that some of the produce was tainted with illegal pesticides," Keisha interrupted before Shane could speak, her fists on her hips and her glare accusing as she confronted Wallaston.

Shane stared directly at Wallaston watching for his reaction, while he snapped pictures with the small camera embedded in a button on his shirt. Jack had leaned forward in his chair waiting for Wallaston to answer.

There was a flash of surprise in his eyes but when Wallaston replied his face was flat and showed no emotion. "That is preposterous," Wallaston said, projecting an attitude of mild confusion. "We wouldn't allow that."

Bob Miller interjected, "Unfortunately, we tested some produce that was delivered under cover of the night, and it definitely does not adhere to current FDA regulations."

Shelley's hands were clasped in front of her on the table. She looked as if she'd aged twenty years in the last day. "The broccoli is from Happy Tummy Farms."

"What do you have to do with this Shelley?" Monica Peterson frowned, or tried to, her brows and forehead barely moved.

"I am co-partner of the farm," Shelley confessed. "And the produce was tainted."

"So you knew about using Aldicarb!" Wallaston accused.

And Shane knew they had him. Because no one had mentioned the specific type of pesticide that had been used on the produce. And Aldicarb was actually approved for use on certain vegetables just not broccoli.

Jack hadn't moved but even Shane could see the tension vibrating off him.

"Well now, Mr. Wallaston." Keisha smiled, and Shane was sincerely happy that shark grin wasn't aimed at him. "No one mentioned what kind of pesticide you purposely used on that produce."

"What are you talking about?"

"I had no idea you authorized this." Shelley jumped up. "This was supposed to be a good thing. And you ruined it."

Tears shimmered in her eyes and Shelley angrily wiped away her frustration.

"Face it, Wallaston. Shelley wouldn't hurt a fly," Keisha said gleefully. "You're going down."

"You can't prove I had anything to do with this," Wallaston snarled. "I'm just the capital guy. I'm not involved in the day to day of the running of the operation. And—"

"Shelley wouldn't have access to Aldicarb," Shane interrupted.

Wallaston calmed, leaned back in his chair, and smiled. It was that same smile he'd given Keisha the other night when he'd noticed her hickey. Smarmy and slick, like he had a secret. "You aren't going to make this public."

Shane raised his brows but stayed silent.

"Why not?" Keisha was sitting right next to Wallaston, her hands loose and open by her sides, but her anger was like a snake coiled around her body.

Suddenly the vibe in the room turned ugly.

"The negative publicity would be deadly." Wallaston smirked some more. "Food for Life can't afford to make it known that they almost distributed tainted produce."

And fuck him, but he was correct. The resulting publicity would damage their credibility and they'd lose donations. In the end the recipients of the food they collected would be the losers. But damn, Shane wanted to nail this guy. As Shane watched Keisha he knew she felt the same.

"Luckily we didn't distribute any of your produce," Bob Michaels said. "You could have caused thousands to be ill."

Shelley had jumped up to pace the carpet. "You destroyed the soil."

"It would have been fine."

"So, *Don*," Keisha emphasized his first name, and Shane

wanted to chuckle. She knew that her familiarity was going to piss the guy off. "How did those chemicals end up on that produce?"

Smart. She was smart. They didn't have enough right now to nail him. They needed him to give details so that Shelley would be exonerated, even if the only people who knew what happened were in this room.

"I had an old order at one of my other farms that somehow never got destroyed. I just ordered the acceptable sprays for Happy Tummy Farms, and then switched them. I couldn't use Aldicarb on the produce that my corporate farms sells."

His tone was perfectly reasonable, as if he wasn't discussing poisoning thousands of unwitting people who got their food from the food bank.

"You jackass," Keisha burst out.

Wallaston shoved back his chair, and Shane went on high alert. He didn't like the look in Don Wallaston's eyes.

Shane and Keisha also stood up, ready to restrain Wallaston if necessary.

"Everyone calm down," Jack said authoritatively.

Bob Miller stood. "Really Don? You would jeopardize the health and welfare of the people we are trying to serve."

"At least they won't go hungry," he snarled. "Isn't that the point?"

"Because a full belly with cancer is better than an empty one?" Keisha jerked her head back, and as the asshole tried to justify his actions, Shane could literally see the rage in her swell until it breached the damn that held back her emotions.

"It was a fucking business decision." Wallaston's face was mottled and a fine sheet of sweat covered his red cheeks. But Shane didn't like the way his gaze darted around the room, looking for a way out of his predicament. Shane could practically feel Wallaston's sense of being trapped.

Suddenly Wallaston grabbed Keisha, his beefy arm wrapped around her neck and yanked her back against his body. Which would have been nothing but Wallaston had a gun. Held right against Keisha's temple.

Shane's heart stopped.

A weapon in the hands of an unstable subject was a nightmare.

Shit.

Shane wanted to panic. But dammit there wasn't time. And if it had been just him and there hadn't been innocent civilians in the room, he'd have attempted to disarm the guy immediately. But the weapon was way too close to Keisha's head. And Shane was intimately acquainted with the deadly effect of a round fired at close range.

Sweat sheened on his forehead. But then he looked at Keisha. All those feelings he'd tried to avoid, getting too close to a woman, keeping his heart safe, had disappeared when Wallaston put that weapon to her temple.

He'd been fooling himself. He'd been half in love with her for months. He loved her mood swings, loved her colorful outfits, and her sass. He wanted her to know she could trust him. He wasn't going anywhere. But he also knew it was going to take her time to believe.

All that hit him in an instant. He needed to save her so they could have that time. So that she could learn to trust him. And he could fall all the way in love with her.

That amazing epiphany was cut short when Shane stared into her amazing hazel eyes and without words, she begged him to trust her.

She wasn't going to let him save the day.

She'd been in the Navy. She was a total ball buster, and

he knew she had skills. Jack wouldn't have hired her if she hadn't. "It's okay," she said calmly. Her sass and attitude nowhere to be seen.

"Bob, why don't you get everyone out of here," Shane directed.

"No." Wallaston's arm tightened on Keisha's neck and Shane fought the urge to go for his gun. His 9mm weighted down his ankle like an anchor.

Keisha may be loud and quick to jump in and take control when she was threatened personally but when she was at work she was rock solid, and this was work. She wasn't about to blow this.

So Shane was acceding to her silent request to let her handle this.

Keisha tried to disrupt Don Wallaston's plan of action or non-plan because what idiot would try to take a woman hostage in this small, tight space? She had to throw him off his game. "So, Don, why donate the produce anonymously?"

He sighed as if suffering from the idiocy of these questions. "We couldn't have that produce associated with the non-profit farm. Later once all the broccoli had been delivered and we were delivering new produce we could switch to a regular delivery schedule so we could take advantage of the tax write off. But I should have known that Shelley couldn't do this one thing right."

"So you authorize the use of a dangerous pesticide on food for those who can't provide for themselves, and I'm the one who can't do anything right?" Shelley's voice rose shrilly.

It was the opening that Keisha had been waiting for. She grabbed Wallaston's wrist, pointed the weapon at the ceiling, yelled at everyone, "Get down." Then rammed her head back into his nose.

He howled as his cartilage crunched. Keisha twisted and with a precision move, she disarmed him, weapon in her hand and pointed at the floor. With one more move, she turned Wallaston around and pressed him up against the wall of the conference room, his arm twisted up his back.

"Nice work, Mrs. Washington." Jack teased.

"I could use a little help." Keisha shot Shane a look.

"Even if you revealed the fact that we used the pesticides, it's only a fine. Nothing that Shelley can't afford to pay," Wallaston sneered, still believing he had the upper hand. "You've got nothing on me personally."

"Well now, that would be true." The glee in Keisha's voice was unmistakable. "Except you just threatened a roomful of people with a loaded firearm."

Wallaston snorted. "You won't do it."

"Try me, asshole." With his confession and the attempted use of violence, Wallaston might not go down for using the illegal pesticides but he was in big trouble. Assuming the board decided to press charges. And she really, really hoped they did.

All the other board members stood stock still, staring at Keisha as if they'd never seen a kick ass woman before.

Monica Peterson's mouth was hanging open in a display she'd no doubt find inappropriate if she'd been thinking about it.

"Way to go, babe," Shane said huskily. He removed the weapon from her hand, and then pulled some zip ties from his pocket.

Mission accomplished.

CHAPTER 9

The sting was over. The police had arrested Wallaston for carrying concealed and brandishing a weapon in public. Shelley was clearly wracked with guilt. "I just wanted to do a good thing."

The case, at least their piece of it, was for all intents and purposes wrapped.

Keisha had gone through a thousand emotions today. She was wrung out mentally and still had physical aches from the last two nights of energetic sex. And whoa she did not need her mind to go there.

"So I guess this means there is no donation," Monica Peterson said glumly.

Bob Miller responded quickly, "If we'd distributed that food and word had gotten out, we'd be short donations everywhere. Their time and getting to the bottom of the mystery was the donation."

Keisha shot a narrowed gaze at Jack. This whole 'married couple who are going to donate a lot of money' sham was his idea, he should donate the money. She

79

propped her fist on her hip and silently sent him a 'you'd better do this' message.

He shrugged.

"Actually." Shane placed his hand on Keisha's shoulder .The first time he'd touched her since this morning and she jolted. "Washington Aviation will be making the donation."

"Really?" Monica and Keisha said at the same time.

"Keisha and I were very impressed with your operation. Not to mention the fact that you jumped right on top of a potential problem before it could become a serious one."

He made it sound like they were a couple. What the hell was he doing? Could he really afford to give them such a large donation? And why did she care? But her heart melted a little at his generosity.

Shane continued, "Listen, when I was growing up, my family could have been one of the families in need. Now that I have the means, I'd like to help."

"Thank you so much." Monica placed her perfectly manicured hand on his forearm. And Keisha fought the urge to growl. She was standing right next to Shane! And she was pretty sure Monica Peterson who was old enough to be Shane's…aunt at the very least, thought she and Shane were married.

As if he could feel her ire rising. Shane slung his arm around Keisha's shoulder and she was so incensed that she didn't even object to his claiming.

"You're welcome." Shane tugged her toward the door. "Let's get out of here."

"I figured I would get a ride with Jack." It was time to start protecting her heart. Shane Washington was a compelling, mesmerizing man and she'd lived under his spell for the past few days but now it was time to get back to her real life.

"Sure," Jack began.

Shane shook his head at Jack.

After one raised, scarred eyebrow, and a speculative glance between the two of them, Jack said, "Ah, actually I need to get Shelley home. She's going to have a lot of work to get Happy Tummy Farms ready for their next crop."

Shane had just cock blocked her.

"I'll give you a ride." He grinned, his lips upturned and his teeth gleamed white. Keisha wondered if anyone else heard the sexual insinuation beneath his simple words.

She thought about arguing but she could tell by his insistence, she wasn't going to get rid of him that easily.

"Fine." She strolled past him as if going with him were her idea.

As they exited the food bank's office, Shane told Monica Peterson, "My accountant will be in touch."

"Thank you again, Mr. Washington," she gushed.

"Call me Shane."

"You want me to wait outside while you have a moment?" Keisha grumbled under her breath.

Shane's arm was still slung around her neck and his muscles tensed slightly. "See you later, Monica."

Shane hustled Keisha to his car, almost as if he was afraid she was going to run away.

"What's the hurry?" she sniped.

"I want you alone," Shane said huskily, his voice low and deep, the sound rumbled through her body where they touched. "I told you what I wanted to do to you once this was over."

Keisha's heart thudded fast and sharp against her breastbone. "That's not a good idea."

"You're right."

Irrational disappointment hit her. Which told her she

really needed to get away from Shane before he squashed her heart beneath his size fifteen loafers.

"It's a great idea."

Shane started the car, then pealed out of the parking lot. They rode in silence for a while, Keisha staring out the window at the mid-afternoon traffic on Highway 1 until she realized they were traveling south, away from her condo.

"You're going the wrong way."

"No. I'm not." Shane's hand was loose on the wheel.

For some reason, his calm delivery sparked a mini panic. "I thought you were going to take me home."

"Maybe I am."

She mulled over his response. "I really don't need to see your bachelor pad."

He snorted. "I'm thirty-eight years old. I don't have a bachelor pad. I have a home."

That shut her up. She didn't want to fall any further under his spell. She'd go see his home and then get the hell out of there. Protect herself, and her heart at all costs.

Shane wanted to growl in frustration. He'd lost her again. He could literally feel her pulling away from him and mentally retreating to the other side of the car.

As much as he wanted her, he didn't think keeping her in thrall with sex and distracting her from real life was the right method for getting her to stay.

He exited the highway and took the turn toward his house. Maybe he could charm her with his view.

"Are you sure you are okay with the donation to the food bank?" she said out of the blue. "Really, Jack should be donating that money. He's the one who asked for the favor."

"It's not a problem."

She frowned, as if she didn't believe him.

He continued patiently, "I own my own business. I own

a small plane but most of the planes I fly for business are owned by my clients, so my overhead is low. I get paid every time I take a trip for the client and they also foot the bill for my lodging and food." Not to mention he'd invested in SAE, Jack's father's company years ago. It had been a wise choice.

"Okay." She shook her head and her curls brushed the exposed curve of her neck. He really wanted to lean over the gearshift and lick that spot until she purred. But he had to restrain himself.

If he used sex right now, she'd never believe that he was interested in more. And he was very, very interested in more.

Shane pulled up across from his duplex. There was quick access to the beach path here.

"I love this beach." Keisha exited the car, tossed her heels on the passenger seat, and headed for the shoreline.

Shane smiled as she barreled down the path and onto the sand. She stretched her arms toward the sky, tilted her head back, and lifted her face to the cool afternoon sun.

After he removed his own socks and shoes, he followed her onto the beach. "You like the ocean?"

"No duh, why do you think I joined the Navy?"

Shane's laugh rumbled through him, happy to see her former sass back. Just because he loved her sweet didn't mean he didn't want that sass too.

He picked her up and twirled her around like she was a little kid.

"What are you doing, you nut. Put me down," she demanded but her face was wreathed in a big smile.

Shane whirled her around one more time, then gently settled her on her feet. He turned her so she faced the sea and wrapped his arms around her waist. Then he rested his chin on her shoulder.

The waves crashed against a collection of large rocks

about thirty feet out. Sea lions bellowed and seagulls squawked as wind whipped through the corridor and white sea foam crashed against the brown sand. Long strings of kelp lay in ropes on the beach, and the salty briny sea perfumed the air.

They stood there in silence, both seemingly hesitant to interrupt the feeling of communion. Shane felt a peace settle over him. Sweet and sass and the ability to recognize the need for a quiet moment. "I never get tired of this view."

"You come here often?"

"I live across the street."

She turned around and peered at his duplex. The houses were close together, sacrificing some privacy for the view, but he didn't care.

"Wow."

"Not as fancy as Jack's."

"Nothing's as fancy as Jack's house," she said drily.

She stared back at the house. At the two doorways next to each other. "Who lives on the other side?" Her gaze shot to him, eyes wide as if she already knew.

"My mama." It had been one of the proudest moments of his life when he'd been able to give his mother a home.

"Doesn't that get a little restrictive when you have… friends over?"

"Why are you being so polite?" he growled. "Just ask what you want to."

"Okay, screw polite." Keisha tossed her head. "Isn't uncomfortable when you have women sleep over?"

"No it's never been restrictive because I don't invite women to my home." Shane curled his palms around her shoulders to keep her attention on him. "Ever."

"Oh." She pressed her lips together and tried to shift away from him, turn around to face the sea again.

She wasn't getting it. He was going to have to lay it all on the line and hope she didn't crush him. Because he had hope. More than he'd ever had. He'd never wanted a woman, in every aspect, the way he wanted Keisha.

"So, you want to come inside?"

"Me?" Keisha held very still as if listening to some internal voice. "I don't think that's a good idea. I should probably get going."

"What?"

"I don't believe I stuttered." Keisha snarked at him. "I should get going."

"You're refusing my invitation."

"I'm sure you'll get over it." Keisha broke his light hold and headed toward the car. "By tonight would be my guess."

Shane didn't get angry. Ever. Someone his size always had to be in control or bad things could happen but he was seriously close to losing it now. Shane grabbed her arm, stopped her in her tracks, forced her to turn and look at him.

What he wanted to do was crush his mouth to hers and grind her into submission with sex. But that was a temporary solution to the larger problem. He could probably get her to stay at his house for a few hours but once they'd slaked their sexual hunger, he'd be right back in the same position. Trying to convince her to take a chance on him.

"Believe in me. Believe in us." Shane wasn't used to begging, ever, but for this strong woman, he had to make her listen. "Take a chance. I promise to try to never let you down."

She rolled her eyes. She didn't believe.

Shane knew he was going to have to lay it all on the line. Have to show her a side of himself that no one had ever seen. He had to put it out there because he couldn't imagine a day without her in it. "You once asked me why I used to play the field."

He hoped she'd catch the past tense.

"My mother never got over losing my dad. It was easier and safer to keep it light, surface, temporary." Shane knew that wasn't going to be enough. It was all or nothing. He took a deep breath. So many had let Keisha down, he figured he needed to be completely honest and he needed to show her the vulnerability that had lived in his heart for years.

Shane took another deep breath then plunged. "Forever comes with a lot of pain."

Keisha's heart thundered against her breastbone. It had not escaped her attention that Shane had said, he *used to* play the field. Did that mean he was stopping? And how could she ever trust that?

But his seeming sincerity tugged at her. "What does forever have to do with me?" She had to ask. Had to.

"You make me want to try forever. And I'm ready to risk it."

"Why are you doing this? Can't you let this little fling die a normal death?" She shot the questions at him to cover her own terror. She wanted to believe him. Wanted to believe they could have forever. But there hadn't been a whole lot of forever in her life. Actually there had never been anything close to forever.

"You…infuriate me."

"That's a good reason to break your pattern for the last thirty eight years." The sass was back and she couldn't help

the pang of hurt because that wasn't what she'd wanted to hear.

Wait no, that wasn't right. She didn't want to hear any reason that convinced her to take a chance on him. Even though she wanted that chance, with every breath in her body, and every stupid hope in her heart, she wanted to take a chance on him. On them.

"You invigorate me. You inspire me to be a better man than I am. You turn me on. You got me to have sex with you in the back of my freaking car."

She flushed and a deep rose spread over her cheeks.

"I've never even been tempted and there I am twisted into a pretzel with my pants around my thighs and you laid out beneath me like a gift."

"So we have sexual chemistry," she said, still trying to stop him.

"I love how sweet you get when you're looking out for someone. I love that gooey, soft center that you cover up with tough." Her gooey soft center was melting at his sweet words and it was getting harder and harder to resist him.

"Well that center doesn't appear too often."

"I know, but I love watching for it."

Keisha wanted to believe him, but what about a week from now? A month from now? When the new and fantasy had worn off and he was sick of her. "I'm rarely sweet. I'd just as soon kick your ass."

"I love your sass. I love your drive. I love how you kicked Wallaston's ass today." Shane continued, "I love how you were ready to go to war with Jack over that donation. I love that you were looking out for me."

"I'm sure you'd get tired of that sass right quick," she countered.

"I love you," he roared.

As the surprise confession burst from him in a rush, he knew it was true. He'd fallen for this crazy, sweet, hot, sassy woman. And while the idea was scary as hell, he didn't want to walk away. He wanted her. Forever.

Keisha blinked, her mouth in a rounded O of surprise. To be truthful, he'd surprised himself.

Keisha's heart was thundering in her chest. The words had burst from him like uncontrollable emotional vomit. And she knew in that moment, he meant them. But how long would that love last before he was tired of her?

"Keish. Trust in me," he said, if he knew exactly what she was thinking. "You trusted me earlier."

He was right. In that conference room, he could have rushed Wallaston. Instead he trusted Keisha to do her thing and she had trusted him to let her.

"I won't let you down." Shane vowed.

"Don't you think you'll get tired of just me? You're a player." But she said the words like a shield. Even she wasn't sure she believed them anymore.

Shane thought about his mother. "My mother told me a long time ago, that she may not have had my father for long but he made such an impact that no one else has ever come close to making her feel the same way."

"Your mother was extremely lucky then."

And Shane realized in that instant that he hadn't been avoiding love, he'd just never found anyone who made a big enough impact. "I listened to those words, Keisha. But now I've found you. You're my impact."

"Oh." Keisha's body softened against his. And a joy thundered in his chest. He had her. "That's so…sweet."

Shane held his breath. He knew from their past discussions about life and their own viewpoints that their relationship wasn't going to be perfect. But they'd have plenty of time to get it right.

"Okay," she finally said.

"Okay…?"

"You going to show me your home or what?" With her hand propped on her hip and her curls brushing her shoulder, the sass was back. And he knew what she really meant was she loved him too.

THANK you for reading Shane and Keisha's story, Jar of Hearts! I hope you loved getting to know these characters just as much as I have. If you did enjoy this novella, below are a few ways you can help a writer out!!

GOOD: Lend the book to a friend

BETTER: Recommend the book to your friends

BEST: Leave a review at Apple, Amazon, BN, Goodreads, All Romance...basically any place they sell eBooks. Every review helps my work get out to other readers and I cannot even express how much it means to me when you let people know you liked my work. Readers have so many choices nowadays and limited dollars to spend. It can be difficult to take a chance on a new author even if the premise sounds appealing. By reviewing books, you give other readers insight into the story world and help them make informed purchases.

· · ·

THANK YOU, thank you, thank you for your support!!

P.S. Would you like to know when my next book is available? You can sign up for my new release email list/newsletter at Lisa's Confidants

Welcome to the world of the Stone Family siblings, Jess, Connor, Riley and Jack. I hope you loved getting to know the Stone siblings as much as I did. In the course of writing the four interconnected books, I developed quite an affection for both Keisha, who we meet in Stone Cold Heart, and Shane who we meet in Heart of Stone. And then we get to know both of them a little better in Still The One.

Jar of Hearts was supposed to be a short story of the relationship between Keisha Johnson, an employee at GHR and Stone Consulting, and Shane Washington, the on call pilot for the company.

But Keisha and Shane wouldn't let me alone and their story blossomed into a novella. The Food for Life food bank is fictional but the information and details about the operations and the distribution is similar to my local food bank where my family has volunteered for the past few years.

EXCERPT FROM STONE COLD HEART

Family Stone #1 Jess

In the early evening dusk, Jess Stone lay on her stomach in the twenty foot high rubble of a demolished church, underneath a black and gray city-scape tarp intended to camouflage her position. A sharp-edged chunk of debris dug into her lower rib cage, the scope of the Remington M24 cool and familiar against her face.

Her standard uniform of jeans, running shoes, and plain black t-shirt rendered her just another anonymous and transient relief worker...which she was actually. A black baseball cap hid her distinctive multi-hued blonde hair. The paper mask kept out the contaminated dust from the destroyed buildings but did little to stem the overwhelming stench of decaying bodies.

Tanks rumbled through the destroyed coastal town, their public address system blasting warnings for citizens to stay in their homes, curfew was in effect. The threat was a joke. Ninety percent of the people in the town didn't have homes left. Those who did were terrified to go back inside. In the fetid, humidity choked air, the tent cities erected in the parks and on the beach were seething masses of the injured and shock struck.

The substandard construction in the small country had never been enough to withstand the angry might of Mother Nature. Buildings had toppled like a stack of Tinkertoys, and left crumbling cement walls with twisted rebar poking out of the jagged ruins like a skeletal hand.

Trapped in the concrete pieces that littered the ground, the heat from the tropical day seared through her thin sturdy clothing. The stank of the raw sewage that ran in rivulets through the streets overpowered the salt-laden breeze off the ocean. People, covered with the grit of pulverized buildings and humans, shuffled along with blank vacant stares. Two weeks after the quake, still in shock, their lives decimated first by nature and then kicked and beaten by the ineffectiveness of a flawed relief system. Hundreds of humanitarian agencies had descended on the population duplicating efforts and yet completely missing the need in other areas. The government was ostensibly trying to coordinate the effort, however the mass chaos was undeniable.

Through the Leupold Ultra M3 fixed power sight, she tracked the movements of Henri LeRoy, leader of this tiny island nation, violator of human rights and dignity, and all around poor excuse for a human being.

Sickness roiled in her stomach. The power bar she'd eaten for breakfast threatened to add to the rubble pile as she tried to figure out how in the hell she'd ended up here. Back behind a sniper rifle with the power over life and death trembling in the muscles of her right trigger finger.

Dammit. When she'd decided to take control of her life and quit the FBI, she hadn't wanted to do this anymore.

She'd wanted to be a simple relief worker. She'd wanted to connect with her family, brothers and mother.

But that bitch, fate, had slapped her upside the head and now here she was, where she'd sworn she never wanted to be again. Looking through the scope of a high-powered rifle, with a crystal clear head shot and a murky sense of right and wrong.

With little fanfare, she could blast LeRoy's brain matter all over the silk-covered walls and the antique Louis the XIV scrolled chairs in the receiving room of his ridiculously elegant weekend mansion which, since built properly, had sustained minimal damage. Her muscles twitched with the knowledge and acceptance that with one slow slide of her finger, the despotic, amoral leader would be history.

Jess didn't want to kill him, didn't want to be directly responsible for another death. She didn't want this choice. She'd given up this kind of life. She'd left the FBI after a series of high stress cases to get away from the doubt and guilt that had crippled her. To make her own decisions about right and wrong rather than carry out the commands of her bosses.

But if Henri LeRoy lived, chances were astronomical that many other citizens would die.

And yeah, she'd probably been manipulated into this. Actually no probably about it. Assassination had not been listed as one of her duties when she'd joined Global Humanitarian Relief. Damn her brother anyway.

But now all she could do was lay here in the desecrated remains of the former church and hope that her special skill set wouldn't be needed.

Fortunately, she was secondary backup.

And unless several things went horribly wrong, she would break down her weapon, get back to the relief aid encampment, back to actually helping people, and be out of here without ever firing her rifle.

Then she could hand out seed packets to her heart's content and figure out what she was going to do next. If she'd stay with GHR and her brothers, or go. First, she had to get through the next two hours.

But if something did go wrong...she prayed that if she was called upon, she could make the right decision. Make the shot. Cold zero.

EXCERPT FROM BLOWBACK

Blowback (blo′ bak) *n.* A deadly, unintended consequence of a covert operation.

Eerie blue light penetrated my consciousness first. The regulated thump-thump of tires pounded in my head, echoing with fierce resonance.

Where the hell was I? Why did I feel like this? I kept my eyes closed, knowing pretense was paramount to my survival. Wherever I was, it wasn't normal.

Ha. My life would never be normal.

I tracked back to my last memory. I'd hooked up with a guy. Had relatively indiscriminate sex with him.

I inhaled shallowly, carefully, not wanting to give away anything. I still smelled like sex. Really great sex.

I wanted to smile but kept my expression lax.

I'd longed to stay in that bed. Sleep with him. Just sleep with the comforting warmth of another human being. The ache had been so intense that as soon as he dozed off--I left.

That was my last memory.

"You can stop pretending."

I continued to fake sleep. I didn't know that male voice.

It was bland, not angry, but with a slight smirk, as if he knew something I didn't.

"You should be awake by now. We calibrate our doses very carefully."

That statement raised so many questions, I decided to comply with his unspoken request and let my eyes drift open. I calculated we were moving at a speed of about thirty miles per hour. Suburban, blacked out windows, bulletproof glass. The blue light came from the interior dome in the big SUV.

"The light is to protect your eyes. The drug affects your pupil's ability to dilate and contract."

What drug? I kept silent.

"Not very curious, are you?"

My last conscious memory was from the motel off of 295 near Alexandria around nine in the evening. It was pitch dark out now, so I'd been out for a while.

Lucas. Could the guy have been a plant? Possible. Since he was my last clear memory, it made sense.

I sifted through the spaghetti of my brain. For the past two days, I'd been undercover, shadowing Staci Grant's life. Last night, I'd encountered Lucas Goodman, who'd been looking for Staci and thought he'd found her when he found me. The sexual heat between us had been instantaneous and mutual. A few sweaty hours later, I'd left, confident my movements as Staci had been tracked. My cover had been working.

They'd kidnapped Staci.

Excellent.

I was right where I needed to be.

Now I needed answers. My task was to discover why CIA, DIA, and NSA agents were being kidnapped, the method of interrogation, and who was doing the kidnapping. The answers would be coming. I just had to be ready.

I settled into the backseat of the car to wait, taking in details. Mistake number one. They hadn't taken my ring, so the satellite audio transmitter should work. I twisted the unusual ring with my thumb and pressed the citrine stone twice. I was now sending voice-activated recordings back to Carson.

Mistake number two. They'd cuffed my hands, in front, but left my legs unshackled.

They'd taken my government firearm but missed the knife in the sheath at my waist. Mistake number three. Always, always check everywhere for hidden weapons.

Although my mind was the most powerful weapon I had.

My watch was gone and my government-issue GPS with it. Slouching to the side, I got a better view of the dashboard panel. My kidnapper had conveniently supplied me with another GPS system, live and tracking.

Coordinates. Latitude–47. Longitude–122. I was in the Pacific Northwest. I looked out the misted window to see a reflection of the Space Needle and pinpointed my location as Seattle. I was a long way from Virginia.

I returned my gaze to the kidnapper. Subject was male, small head, blond hair gelled into little spikes, crescent-shaped birthmark below his right ear.

The car rolled to a stop. The rocking intensified my queasy stomach. I ignored it.

"We're here."

Here was a warehouse near the water. The guy wasn't rough but the sudden motion as he lugged me out of the SUV caused my stomach to roil.

I breathed in the cold, damp air through my nose, trying

to quell the nausea. As he led me toward a semi-truck trailer, I noted the parking lot was empty except for one other truck and a car, too far away and too dark to make out details. The warehouse, constructed with long cinder block walls interrupted by doors at twenty foot intervals, was to my left and behind me.

The trailer was modified from a regular shipping container, doors locked up tight in the back, with another entrance on the side. It looked as if the stairs were all one solid block which could fold up into the interior of the trailer.

The recessed entrance looked exactly like an old-fashioned front door complete with screen door. A porch light flicked on. The screen door wheezed open as a dark-haired woman in a white coat stepped out onto the platform.

The light behind her filled the doorway with shadows. I couldn't make out her features but I caught a furtive movement, the light illuminating her hand as she tucked a syringe into her pocket.

"Thank you. You can go now." She nodded regally to the man holding me. Her melodic voice held a hint of Asia, probably second-generation American.

He promptly let go of my arm and walked away. They must believe that the plastic restraint cuffs would be a big deterrent to resistance. The click of his heels echoed in the silence as she stared at me, her hands clasped tightly in front of her, so tightly her knuckles showed white.

There was something in her stance--tension, stress? I eased back a step.

"Welcome." She put a hand on the railing and took a step down. Then she hesitated and glanced back at the open doorway. "We won't hurt you."

I thought about the syringe in her pocket. *No thank you.*

I'd had drug resistance training but honestly I didn't want to put it to the test. At least, not yet. Although if that scenario became unavoidable and they pumped me full of drugs, the transmitter in my ring guaranteed I would get the information Carson and the NSA needed.

All of the kidnapped agents had an unidentified drug in their bloodstream and unknown consequences from those drugs. We had no idea what national secrets they'd given away or what kind of long-term effects were possible from the drug cocktail most likely in that syringe. My job was to get myself kidnapped, acquire the drugs, identify the perpetrators, and get out before they could accomplish their objective.

I wobbled as if unsteady on my feet and eased back two steps, assessing my position.

As the Suburban left, the beam from the head lamps shone on her. The shape of her face and the tilt of her eyes marked her as Chinese. Lines of strain curled around her mouth, the expression was supposed to be a smile but came off as more of a grimace. "Come with me."

I don't think so.

I'd expected the kidnapping, the intel suggested that Staci Grant would be next. I'd planned to resist at first. I didn't want to make it too easy for them to subdue me. Carson was supposed to have a team on standby waiting to capture the kidnappers after I completed my objectives. But since we hadn't planned for a cross country abduction—all of the other kidnappings had been local and accomplished within a matter of several hours—it would most likely take a little time before the extraction team got here.

If they got here.

I pivoted and ran for the warehouse door nearest me. Her footsteps rang on the metal steps as she followed.

"She's getting away." A man's shout, older, deeper, slightly frantic, registered as I reached the door. Two against one. More difficult, but not impossible. Woman, older man. Until I saw his physique, I couldn't judge who was more dangerous.

"I've got it," the woman replied and sprinted toward me.

I yanked on the handle, flung the door open, and slid inside. The heavy metal swung shut with an ominous clang.

Obviously, the drugs were making me melodramatic.

The warehouse was dimly lit. Industrial metal lights hung from the ceiling, their muted pink glow making the surroundings blurry. Metal shelving separated the concrete floor into long, wide aisles. Three tiers of jumbo shelves housed wooden pallets of goods. I stood at the end of one aisle.

I hustled over two aisles, pulling the knife from the sheath at my waist as I went. The restraint cuffs at my wrists took a few swipes before slicing clean through.

I grabbed some small ceramic rice bowls and shoved them into my jacket pockets. Mistake number four. They'd let me keep my jacket.

The door banged open.

"Don't let her escape." I could hear the man huffing, and a rhythmic thumping noise as they pursued.

"She won't escape," the woman replied grimly from somewhere behind me.

I stalked down the industrial cement aisle, my footsteps silent. Glancing around, I searched for another way out.

"Please don't try to escape, Agent Hunt." The man's plea had a desperate edge to it.

My legs faltered. I wanted to stop, stand rooted to the floor. Only training kept me moving.

He'd spoken my real name. My *real* name, not the cover I was using for this assignment. So who did they really want?

Me, Jamie Hunt, NSA agent? Or Staci Grant, CIA officer?

Stone Cold Heart:

Jess Stone, former **FBI** sniper, always felt like the kid who looked in the candy store window but could never afford to go in. But on a humanitarian mission to aid an earthquake ravaged country, finally she finds a place where she fits, in Colin Davies' arms, and working for Global Humanitarian Relief, her big brother's company. But can the former SAS thaw Jess's stone cold heart?

Carved in Stone:

Connor Stone has always been odd man out in his family. Not the oldest, not the most charming, he'd had a lock on the youngest until another half-sibling came to live with them, so he raised hell in his youth. Con knows now the only way to redeem himself is with deeds, not words and sets out to prove once and for all he is worthy of the Stone family. When his older brother asks him to take care of business, Con finally will have redemption he craves. Except when Ava Sanchez, his brother's assistant, is threatened, he must choose between saving the girl or protecting his family. Will his choice bring him love or break his heart?

Heart of Stone:

Riley Stone is the handsome brother, the charming one. Everyone who meets him compares him to his father, which in his mind is not a compliment. But he's never met a woman he couldn't charm, until he meets Di, an acerbic, smart-mouthed, passionate activist who has no time for him or his charm. On the run, in the midst of danger, the blistering passion they share explodes. Can these two opposites find common ground, or will Di smash Riley's stone heart?

Still the One:

Jack Stone, former Navy SEAL, and oldest Stone sibling is determined to keep his family strong. Family is everything. So he starts Global Humanitarian Relief and Stone Consulting to do some good and keep his family together. But when he has to team up with his old flame, Bliss, on a missing persons case, an evil threatens him, his family and the one woman he could never forget and doesn't want to let go. Can these two former lovers put aside past hurts and heal their hearts?

Jar of Hearts:

Prickly Keisha Johnson has the hots for Shane Washington. But she's not about to reveal her inner soft heart to the player pilot and open herself up to hurt, until a favor to their boss sends them undercover and under the covers. Can she trust his sensual attention or will he shatter her fragile heart?

Cold as Stone (John, Family Stone #7)

Family Stone Box Set (Stone Cold Heart, Carved in Stone, Heart of Stone, Still the One, & Jar of Hearts)

The Nostradamus Prophecies

View To A Kill #1

Never Say Never #2

ALIAS

Stalked (ALIAS #1)

Hunted (ALIAS #2)

Vanished (ALIAS #3)

Deceived (ALIAS #4)

Billionaire Breakfast Club

His Semi-Charmed Life (Camp Firefly Falls #11 and Billionaire Breakfast Club #0)

Everything He Wants (Billionaire Breakfast Club #1 The Jock)

Queen of His Daydreams (Camp Firefly Falls #23 and Billionaire Breakfast Club #1.5)

ABOUT LISA

USA Today Bestselling Author Lisa Hughey started writing romance in the fourth grade. That particular story involved a prince and an engagement. Now, she writes about strong heroines who are perfectly capable of rescuing themselves and the heroes who love both their strength and their vulnerability. She pens romances of all types—suspense, paranormal, and contemporary—but at their heart, all her books celebrate the power of love.

She lives in Cape Ann Massachusetts with her fabulously supportive husband, two out of three awesome mostly-grown kids, and one somewhat grumpy cat.

Beach walks, hiking, and traveling are her favorite ways to pass the time when she isn't plotting new ways to get her characters to fall in love.

Lisa loves to hear from readers and has tons of places you can connect with her. It's a wonder she gets any writing done at all....

Sign Up for Lisa's Confidants
Visit Lisa on the Web

Follow Lisa's Boards on Pinterest
Follow Lisa on Instagram
Email Lisa
Be Lisa's Friend on Goodreads
Like Lisa on Facebook at Lisa Hughey: My Books